Securing

Her

Heart

~A NOVEL~

Elizabeth James

Solitaire Series

Book #1

ISBN-10: 0990830810

ISBN-13: 978-0-9908308-1-8

Edited by Kathy Krick

Cover by ShamRock Cover
Designs ©2014

DEDICATION

My two angels, your story will be told…

~with all my love

THANK YOU

To my husband for putting up with this crazy world I've gotten myself into. I appreciate your support and am **still** hoping that one day you'll actually read one of my books! I love you!

Thanks again to my mom and dad for being an amazing support for me my entire life and for giving me a wonderful example of life-long love. I love you both! And thank you to my family for being a pretty awesome bunch! I love you all too!!

To my "sisters", I love you all and thank you for encouraging me to keep on with my dream!

To Kassie Baker, who keeps me grounded, thank you! You've been an amazing friend and "assistant" for all six books now! Thank you for going on this journey with me!

Kathy Krick, you have always done an awesome job. This book challenged me as a writer and yet you still kept me on track. You rock!

To Rochelle who has captured my vision on the cover and brought them to life. Thank you for your unbelievable talent!!

To my beta readers: Kassie Baker, Jodi Negri, Maria DeSouza, Becky Nichols, Rochelle McGrath, and Sharon Courtney…thank you again for your amazing input and suggestions. I hope you like the finished product!

To my fellow authors and fans, thank you for all of your support and I'm so happy to have finally met some of you in person!

To my E. James Street Team: Thank you for all of your support and encouragement throughout the years, I love each and every one of you.

Prologue

It was five in the morning. *Why did they have to have flights leave so early?* I thought to myself as I propped my head against the door and tried to get a few more minutes of sleep in before we got to the airport. My sister, Olivia, had easily fallen back to sleep as soon as we got in the car but even though I tried, I was too excited.

"Jolene, honey? Do you have your passport?" My mom asked from the front seat. "I told you to put it in your bag last night but I know how you are."

I rolled my eyes. "Yeah, Mom. It's in my purse. You worry too much."

She turned to face me. "Jolene Anderson. You are going off to college in another country, for God's sake. Of course I worry!"

My dad laughed and patted her hand. "Jane, she's going to be just fine. You've got to let her grow up sometime."

I touched my hand to my dad's arm. "I love you, Dad," I said smiling at him in the rearview mirror.

"I love you too. Now, did you watch 'Taken' again? I know it's an old movie but it's a wakeup call for young girls in a foreign country." His green eyes sparkled as he grinned at me in the mirror. "I'm no Liam Neeson but I'll come save you if I have to!"

"Yes, I watched it. I promise not to talk to weirdos or even cute guys. This is all about school and I'm totally dedicated to my studying." I heard a sniffle and saw my mom wiping her eyes. "Are you crying, Mom? Please tell me you're not crying. I'm going to be just fine."

Her voice breaking, she said, "I'm just going to miss you, that's all."

I sighed and said, "I'm going to miss you too. I promise to come home every summer."

Olivia woke up on that comment. "What are you guys talking about?" She mumbled as she rubbed her eyes.

I hugged her around her shoulder and said, "My coming home to visit."

She groaned. "You haven't even left yet! Honestly, I'm looking forward to having the bathroom to myself and wearing all the clothes you couldn't take with you."

Sarcastically, I said, "Love you too, sis," with a big smile.

She shook her head and lay it back on my shoulder. "Try to keep it down, there are people sleeping here!" She grumbled.

I really did love my sister and was going to miss her while I was away. Ever since she'd turned thirteen, she'd been coming to me for advice on clothes and boys. Lately, however, she'd become sulky since she found out I was going to college in London, but I assured her we'd stay in touch. I was thankful she'd even wanted to come to the airport with us. My eleven year old brother, Ethan, hadn't. He'd gone on a camping trip with his friends, and even though it hurt my feelings that he didn't want to come, I understood it was just a boy thing. He loved me and was going to miss me, but he definitely wasn't going to let anyone know it.

"Mom," I whispered. "I guess it's too early for Uncle Justin and Aunt Callie to be at the airport, huh?" Although not really related to us, the Brissons had been friends with my parents for years and ever since I was a little girl, I'd called them Aunt and Uncle.

My dad answered, glancing again in the rearview mirror, "I think they were going to try but don't get upset if they don't make it, okay? With such an early flight, you're lucky your sister's even going." Olivia nodded against me in agreement. I'd been hoping they'd be there and bring Ryder and Carter with them. I really wanted to say goodbye to everyone. Dad turned into the airport parking lot, got our ticket stub and found a space not too far from the terminal. I was flying out of Charlotte nonstop to London, which was the way my dad liked it. No way for me to get lost in an airport changing planes and no way for some goons to capture me and sell me into sex slavery. Again, a page from the 'Taken' handbook of traveling.

I shook Olivia awake, which took a minute or two, and finally she sat up and shielded her eyes. "We're here?" She said yawning as she stretched.

I nodded and grabbed my purse and carry-on bag then slipped out of the car. Dad unloaded my bags and easily carried them to the check-in. We were showing my ticket to the valet when I heard my name being screamed across the parking lot.

"JOLENE! Wait for us!" I turned to see Ryder and Carter running across the lanes of traffic followed by their parents. Ryder skidded to a stop next to me, huffing and puffing from his mad dash. "We didn't…want…to…miss saying…goodbye," he panted.

I just shook my head and laughed. "I didn't know for sure you were coming. I'm glad you made it in time." I checked my purse for my passport one more time.

He shrugged. "You know I wouldn't miss it. Who knows when I'll see you again," he said with a smile, his blue eyes sparkling.

Carter stood quietly by with a sad look on his face.

"What's the matter, Carter?" I asked wrapping my arm around his shoulder. He was such a quiet kid, quite the opposite of his outgoing brother.

"I'm gonna miss you, Jolene," he said, his bottom lip quivering.

"Aw, buddy. I'll email you and we can video chat if you want. Plus, I'll try to come home during the summers. It'll be like I never left." I gave him a reassuring squeeze and finally got a tiny smile.

Everyone stood around trying to decide who would start the goodbyes, since they couldn't go through the gates into the actual terminal. Uncle Justin nodded toward my dad. "Jay, it looks like you're going to have to get the ball rolling or she'll never get on the plane." My dad took me in his arms, cleared his throat and said, "Jolene, I love you, Sweet Pea. If you need anything, you know how to get in touch with us." He gave me a tight hug and a kiss on the forehead.

I felt like a little girl again despite being eighteen. I hugged him back and then felt myself being passed off to my mom. "Jolene, you call us as soon as you get there," she said as she tucked a stray curl behind my ear that had escaped from my ponytail. "I'm going to miss you like crazy…and I love you." Her tears started flowing again so my dad pulled her into his arms and held her tightly.

Uncle Justin and Aunt Callie both hugged me at the same time, and I felt her put something in my purse. "Just some spending money," she whispered. "Don't tell your mom."

Olivia was next, giving me her 'I don't care, but I do' hug then with a flip of her long blonde hair, she abruptly turned and walked back to the car to no doubt catch up on some more sleep.

Carter hugged me tightly. "Bye, Jolene," he said before running after Olivia.

Ryder was next and as he nervously ran his hand through his dark unruly hair, it was obvious this was awkward for him. Recently,

I'd overheard my mom talking with Aunt Callie about him having a crush on me, despite my being four years older. He really was a cutie and I felt sorry for the girls in his high school because he definitely was going to be a heartbreaker. With flushed cheeks, he quickly gave me a kiss on the cheek before taking off after his brother.

Shaking my head in amusement, I turned to go into the terminal, then looked back once more to see my parents standing together arm in arm and with a wave, I was on my way.

Chapter 1

Eight years later

Jolene

The plane touched down on the tarmac, and I breathed a sigh of relief. I was home, for good. I pulled my compact from my purse to reapply my lipstick and check my hair. Over eight hours in a tiny seat could do some serious damage, and I wanted to look nice for my family. I tried to conceal the dark circles evident from all the stress I'd been going through but finally gave up. Looking at the reflection in my mirror, I saw a completely different person than the teenager who had left for college with dreams of being a designer. I still had the same deep blue eyes and pale complexion. My brunette hair, which had been a mass of thick curls that hung to my waist, was now straight and cut to my shoulders.

When I'd left for London eight years before, I never imagined staying there so long but the time just slipped away. During the summers that I was able to come home, I'd be so happy to be with my family that I'd mull over the idea of moving back, but then I'd get the itch to return to England, and the idea would fizzle out. This time, I was home for good.

When I arrived in London to attend Fashion College, I never imagined where it would take me. I'd been so lost and scared, but as soon as I got to my dorm and met my roommate, Lucinda Sutcliffe, I felt completely at home. She was from Blackpool, which was in the northern part of England, and she had the most amazing accent. Her long hair was bright red with blonde streaks, and she was tall and thin, towering over me by at least five inches. She had several piercings including one in her tongue and one in her nose. She dressed very eclectically in vintage clothing, which suited her personality perfectly. We became inseparable and within no time, I no longer felt homesick, and instead began focusing on school and my career.

A turning point for me came in my second year of college. I was working on some drawings at the dorm, and Lucinda needed the room for some time alone with her boyfriend, Trevor. I never minded because spending time together was virtually impossible for them since he still lived in their hometown and could only come once a month to visit. I gathered up my tattered sketch pad and pencils and headed to a local coffee shop where I was lucky enough to find a table in the back to spread out my things. Sipping my coffee, I immersed myself in my work, so much so that I never noticed the woman sitting at the table next to me until she spoke.

"Those are stunning," she said. I glanced up to see a beautiful woman with long, jet black hair studying my work. "Are you a designer?" She asked in what sounded to me like an Italian accent.

Laughing, I said, "No, I'm a student. I'm hoping to become a designer…one day."

"Ah," she said pursing her red lips and leaning back in her chair. "What a charming accent. You're an American?"

I nodded. "Yes, I'm from North Carolina. I'm attending college here."

She rose from her table to come stand beside me. "I love your technique. These are very original. You've combined two very different styles and the combination is very striking." She gently traced my lines with her beautifully manicured finger. "You still sketch while everyone else depends on computers, I like that."

I smiled. "Thank you very much, I've always loved to draw." I held out my hand to introduce myself. "Jolene Anderson."

"Giada, Giada Rinaldo," she said holding out her hand.

My mouth fell open, and I dropped my pencil then watched helplessly as it rolled off the table onto the floor." My head was spinning! I was sitting across from the owner and lead designer at the House of Rinaldo!

I finally found my voice. "I know you," I gasped. "I love your designs! My aunt Callie wears some of your things and I've always admired them."

She gave me a dazzling smile. "Then your aunt Callie has good taste, yes?"

This was incredible! I was sitting with Giada Rinaldo. It took me a moment to compose myself. Quickly recovering, I said, "Yes, she does. Oh gosh, I can't believe I'm talking to you! This is amazing!"

"Well," she said pulling a card from her leather Louis Vuitton bag. "I've been looking for the right person to intern with me and I believe fate has brought me to you! Would you be interested in the position?"

My heart was thudding in my chest. What an opportunity! "But…you don't even know me!" I babbled.

She smiled once again and pressed the card into my open palm. "I know something special when I see it. Per favore, come work with me."

I glanced down at the card and gathered the courage to accept. "Of course I will!" I gasped. "This is surreal. I almost feel like I need someone to pinch me to prove it isn't a dream."

She reached up and gave my cheek a gentle pinch. "Be at my design house on Monday afternoon, after your classes, of course. Arrivederci, Jolene." She walked away leaving me staring after her, then back to the card in my hand. When I got back to the apartment and showed Lucinda, she squealed.

"Giada? Oh, you are a lucky one!" She said beaming. "What an opportunity for you!" I called my parents that night and gave them the news. They were so proud of me.

Looking back, that chance meeting led me to one of the most exciting times of my life. As soon as I arrived at the House of Rinaldo, Giada took me under her wing, introducing me to her staff, and she found a small office for me near hers where I could work on whatever came to my mind. When I wasn't in school learning my craft, I was by her side learning everything else. She introduced me to all the top designers, and I sat in the front row with her at every fashion show. It was so exciting and at times exhausting, but I absorbed every bit of their advice that I could.

My school years flew by interspersed with quick trips home for the holidays, and before I knew it, it was time for school to end. My parents flew over for my graduation where I received honors in my class. Afterward, at my graduation dinner, Giada gifted me a permanent position as a designer as well as a bright red sports car. My new job meant I could afford a bigger flat, but I didn't want to live alone, so Lucinda and Trevor, who'd transferred to London, moved into a spacious one overlooking the Thames with me. I still flew home every chance I could get, but as I got busier, the trips home got less frequent. One person I kept missing when I was able to get to the US was Ryder. Our timing was always off and then one summer, I found out he'd joined the Army. I got his address and sent him care packages and I always got a sweet thank you note in return. The next summer, he tried to surprise me with a visit while he was in Germany but unfortunately, I'd flown with Giada to Australia for their fashion week and just missed him. Lucinda met him and gushed about how fit (hot) he was. Although I knew Ryder had always been super cute, I just couldn't imagine him that way, he'd always been like a little kid to me.

Not long after we returned from Australia, Giada introduced me to Marco. Marco Rinaldo was Giada's nephew, and he'd come to London to escape his father's strict household. He was absolutely gorgeous. Olive skin, dark brown hair, vivid green eyes and a rock-hard body were an irresistible combination, and I found myself attracted to him immediately. I was fascinated by his sophistication and his accent drove me wild. I hung on every word, desperate to learn his language, so I could follow his conversations. Not long after arriving, he mentioned wanting to see what London had to offer, and since he wasn't familiar with the city, I eagerly volunteered to show him around. Suddenly having the freedom he'd never experienced before, he went wild. We were out at nightclubs and private parties almost every night. At first, Lucinda and Trevor tagged along with us, but eventually it became just the two of us. Marco was charming, and I fell hard. I truly believed he was the one, and I gave myself to him, body and soul. We became inseparable and soon I was staying at his apartment more than my own dreaming of a future together.

My life was absolutely perfect until the day Giada died. She'd flown to Milan for an important business meeting alone because I'd been taken down by a horrible stomach bug. On the flight back to London, a terrible storm caused the plane to crash in the Swiss Alps, leaving no survivors. The sound of my phone ringing in the middle of the night scared me to death and when I heard the news, I completely shut down. The beautiful, vibrant woman I'd idolized would never be coming back, and I just couldn't accept it. Marco flew out immediately so I was left with Lucinda and Trevor, who tried to console me, but I locked myself in my bedroom. I didn't want to speak to anyone except Marco, but he had to stay in Genoa to comfort his family.

Giada's family held a private memorial service in her hometown, but I couldn't bring myself to climb onto a plane, the fear was so great. I attended the service held in London with my parents who'd come as soon as they heard. Her service was beautiful and she was eulogized by some of her closest friends. Marco, however, stayed with his family in Genoa trying to sort out Giada's complicated affairs, and our only communication was some brief phone calls. A few days later, I forced myself to go back to work after convincing myself that Giada would want me to. Finally, a week later, Marco came back to London, and together we shared our grief, and I'd never felt closer to him.

Weeks passed in a blur and eventually, her will was read. Having never been married and having had no children, she left almost everything to Marco. There was, however, one stipulation in her will for me. She left the rights to my designs exclusively in my name, meaning I controlled some of the most popular designs the House of Rinaldo had ever done. At the office where the attorney concluded the reading of the will, Marco sat stone-faced until he suddenly jumped up from his seat and stalked out of the room muttering Italian expletives under his breath. Confused, I dashed out after him frantically calling his name, but he jumped in his Ferrari, and with tires squealing, left me standing on the sidewalk. Bewildered and in tears, I made my way back to the office where I was forced to call a cab to take me home.

When I arrived at my apartment, he was waiting outside, his jaw clenched as tightly as his fists. Before I could speak, he began gesturing wildly as he shouted, "Why would she give these designs to you? I'm her family!" He snarled. "I should have inherited everything!"

I was stunned. Trying to keep my voice from breaking, I said, "Marco, I worked with her a long time...and she loved me like a part of her family. I didn't force her to do this! They were my designs and I worked so hard on them! Honestly, I'd rather have her here!" I burst into tears and ran upstairs to my flat. As I threw myself onto my bed, I heard Marco's car roar away. I never heard from him again. A few days later, his attorney informed everyone by e-mail that Marco was going to dissolve the company and sell off the designs. The attorney singled me out informing me that Marco had intended to fight the clause relating to me but after consulting with his legal team, he reluctantly agreed to let it go. My heart was broken. I couldn't believe the man who'd become such an important part of my life had turned into a greedy stranger overnight. A few weeks later, I heard that he'd left London and had flown back to Italy. My life was shattered. After the firm was dissolved, I received tons of offers from other designers but just couldn't bear the thought of working with someone else. With a lot of thought, I decided it was time to go home to North Carolina and regroup. A tearful Lucinda saw me off at the airport, and I sadly said goodbye to a life I'd known for so many years, hoping I'd be able to shake some of my grief and pain and start anew. It was time to move on.

The plane stopping with a jolt brought me back from my reflections as it rolled up to the jetway. I quickly touched up my lipstick with my signature Ruby Woo Red. I kicked off my slippers to slide my feet into my pumps. As I leaned over to ease my shoes all the way on, I glanced to my left and saw a man sitting across the aisle giving me an appreciative nod and smile which I returned. A moment later, the door opened and passengers began to push themselves into the aisle to exit the plane. I waited patiently for them to clear out, and then I grabbed my carry-on and made my way off the plane. I took the opportunity to text my dad that I had landed, and he replied that they were already waiting for me. After retrieving my luggage, I passed through customs then out into the airport. I scanned the crowd for familiar faces, and then my eyes caught a six foot banner being held by my family and friends. '*Welcome home, Jolene!*' was emblazoned across it, and I noticed passersby stopping to watch my homecoming. My mom ran toward me, arms outstretched with tears streaming down her cheeks. She grabbed me into a bear hug and held on tightly. "I've missed you so much," she whispered against my hair. "My little girl is finally home to stay." She held me at arms-length and took in my appearance. "You've straightened your lovely curls! Why would you do that?"

"I still have my curls," I said laughing. "I just used my straightener. I promise they're right back every time I wash it." It was nice to be back home with my family, and I knew this was the right place to be. Olivia ran forward to hug me tightly. "I'm so glad you're home, sis!" She was twenty-one now and had grown out of her teens into a beautiful young woman. She'd cut her hair into a shoulder-length style which made her look even more sophisticated. "I love your hair and…oh my God, I love those shoes! Did you bring me a pair?"

When I nodded yes, she just gazed at them with a huge grin on her face.

My little brother, Ethan, was next, but he wasn't so little any more. Towering over me, despite my four inch heels, he hugged me tightly. Aunt Callie and Uncle Justin gave me their group hug, and then I looked around for Carter but hoping that Ryder was there as well.

"They're not here, sweetie," Aunt Callie said patting my shoulder. "Carter is in the playoffs with his baseball team and Ryder is in Afghanistan but is due back at Ft. Bragg this month."

"I had no idea he was there!" I blurted. "I thought he was in Europe somewhere!"

"He wasn't able to tell anyone exactly where he was over there," Uncle Justin said as he took my carry-on from me. "He's getting out of the military not long after he gets back."

I was speechless. I'd received cards from him and not once did he mention he was somewhere dangerous.

As we walked out to the parking lot, Ethan walked up beside me, threw his arm around my shoulder and looking down at me said, "So, what are the European ladies like? I'm thinking of doing the whole college thing over there."

I looked up at my baby brother and laughed. "Ethan, you don't just 'do the college thing'. You have to have a goal and Mom and Dad aren't going to just let you find yourself over in Europe. I had a plan when I left. Do you have one?"

He gave me a half-grin. "You'll laugh if I tell you."

I stopped and looked at him. "Why would you think I'd laugh?"

He shrugged his shoulders. "I don't know."

We continued walking to keep up with everyone. "Ethan, I know I haven't been around much for you guys but I promise that whatever you decide to do with your life, I'll be right there to help you. And I would never think it was stupid!"

He grinned sheepishly. "I want to go to culinary school in Paris." He winced as if waiting for the expected outburst of laughter.

I shook my head and smiled. "A chef? You want to be a chef? Ethan, that's amazing!"

My dad, who was loading my bags in the van grinned and said, "He cooks for us all the time. He's really good! Check out my expanding waistline to see how well he's doing." He patted his slightly rounder stomach.

"Thanks, Dad," Ethan said before climbing in the van. "They let me experiment on them a lot. Last night I made Coq au Vin. It turned out pretty good, if I say so myself."

We got settled in and began the short trip back to my parent's house. I'd bought a two bedroom, two bath condo downtown but I had no furniture, so until I could get out and shop I was going to be staying with them. Olivia was unusually quiet during the drive so I poked her in the arm. "Hey kid, are you going to come help me pick out some things for my new place tomorrow?"

She perked up immediately. "Sure! I'd love to."

"Mom, you're welcome to come shopping with us too," I said as I touched my mom's shoulder gently then gave it a squeeze.

"Thanks, honey, but your dad and I have a spa day planned. You girls have fun." She placed her hand on his, and I saw a look of love pass between them that was so beautiful. I almost cried. Their love was so real and so pure and after having been through my breakup with Marco, I knew it hadn't really been love. I could only pray that one day I'd find a love like that.

Chapter 2

Ryder

I signed the last batch of paperwork which ended my four years in the Army and let out a deep breath. Although I'd enjoyed most of it, I was ready to get out and back to civilian life again.

"Hey, Brisson!" I turned to see my best friend, Seth Foust, sauntering down the hallway. "You're coming over tonight, right?"

Seth and his wife, MaryBeth, had invited me over for a cookout as a getting out/moving away celebration.

"Sure, seven right?" I asked as I slapped him on the shoulder. "Anything I need to bring?"

He laughed. "Just yourself, man. MaryBeth has everything taken care of."

"Your wife is pretty freakin' awesome. I don't know how she takes care of four kids."

He stopped and looked at me seriously. "I only have three kids."

Laughing, I said, "I included you in that number, man. Seriously, I hope I can find a woman like her one day." I smiled and held the door open for him. "She's too good for your ass, that's for sure."

He nodded and grinned. "You're so right. I am way out of my league. It's all good, though. She loves me just the way I am."

"Well, I've said it before, you're a lucky man, Seth," I said as I climbed on my motorcycle. "I'll see you guys in a little while." He waved as I drove out of the parking lot to head back to my nearly empty apartment. I'd already shipped most of my stuff back to Charlotte where it was sitting in storage until I could get there and move it into my new place. Climbing off my bike, I opened the door and tossed my keys onto the counter. My cell phone started ringing, and I looked to see it was my mom.

"Hey, what's up?" I asked as I rummaged around in my half empty fridge.

"We were wondering if you have any idea when you'll be here tomorrow."

I found a can of Coke in the back of the fridge and popped the top before taking a huge swallow. "I'm planning on leaving around noon." I was basing my departure time on how much of a hangover I was going to have in the morning. "Seth and MaryBeth are having me over for a cookout and I'll probably crash at their place tonight."

"Ryder, don't you drink too much," she said with a sigh. "I know you're a grown man but I still don't like it."

"I know." My mom could say things that made me feel like a little kid again. "I'll only have a few beers. And I won't drive, I promise."

"Okay, and thank you. You know I love you and would hate for anything to happen to you."

"I know. Thanks, Mom."

"Oh by the way. Guess who's in Charlotte again?" She asked.

I plopped down on the air mattress in the middle of the living room. "Not a clue. Someone I should know?"

"Well, yes!" She sounded annoyed. "You know her very well. Jolene's back."

At the mention of Jolene, my heart skipped a beat. I'd always had feelings for her, but the fact that I was younger than her by a few years seemed to be an obstacle. Being in Europe and so close to where she was, I got the courage to try to visit her, but unfortunately, my timing was off. Her roommate, Lucinda, had been so nice, and I ended up visiting with her and her boyfriend, Trevor, for a little while before reporting back to the base.

I tried to sound nonchalant. "So, is she visiting?" I asked pretending to yawn.

"No," my mom said. "She moved back about a month ago."

"What would make her do that?"

"Well, a lot has happened. Too much to go into now. We'll tell you all about it when you get here."

"Okay, I'll see you guys around three or four tomorrow afternoon. I love you."

"I love you too, Ryder. Be safe. I know you're riding that motorcycle and I won't stop worrying until you're here."

"I'll do my best. G'night Mom."

I hung up the phone and lay back on the mattress. Jolene was back in Charlotte. This was an interesting development, for sure.

Later that night, I arrived at Seth's house and saw several cars parked in his driveway and his yard. As I walked up to the house I could hear music blaring and as I rounded the corner I was hit with a big "SURPRISE!"

Several of the guys I'd been deployed with were there along with their wives or girlfriends. Seth greeted me with a beer and a plate holding a huge hamburger. "Here, Ryder, plant yourself somewhere and eat up. There's plenty more where that came from!"

I found a lawn chair and plopped down, balancing my plate on my knee and setting my beer on the ground beside me. Several kids were bouncing on the trampoline while a couple of the wives watched to make sure no one ended up doing a header off the side. MaryBeth came up beside me and resting her hand on my shoulder said, "You need a few of those, Ryder. They're a lot of work but they're worth every minute of it."

"Do you mean wives or kids," I joked.

She popped me in the back of the head. "Smartass. Kids, of course. You need a Mini-Me of your own."

I looked over at their three kids who were the perfect mix of the two of them and nodded. "Yeah, I'd like that...one day. I just need to be with the right person."

"Well, you haven't met me yet," a voice said from behind me. I turned to see a tall, gorgeous blonde wearing a blue jean mini skirt and a bright yellow tube top standing behind me. "I'm looking for Mr. Right and it sounds like you're looking for me."

MaryBeth groaned and rolled her eyes. "Debbie, you aren't getting your claws in this one. He's leaving tomorrow for good and I'd like him to leave in one piece."

"Oh, MaryBeth," she drawled. "Look at those blue eyes...I'm in love!" She turned on a dazzling smile. "You're going to have him thinking I'm some sort of tramp. I can assure you, I'm not but I can be if you want me to be."

MaryBeth laughed. "Seriously? You've slept with at least four guys that are here tonight. Let it go, Debbie. Please. And by the way, who invited you anyway?"

Debbie turned on the innocent look and pouted her bright red lips. "You're no fun and you know too much. Obviously, someone's been talking."

MaryBeth shook her head and sighed. "Everyone knows you're a barracks bunny and you set your sights on any single soldier you see. However, this is one you won't be getting."

Debbie huffed then sauntered away, and I couldn't help but laugh. "Thanks, MaryBeth. You saved me from a night of meaningless sex and debauchery. I owe you."

MaryBeth grinned. "Don't mention it. You didn't need the hassle especially with you leaving. We do want to stay friends with you and remember, you can't turn a ho into a housewife."

Seth came by carrying another case of beer, but he stopped to give MaryBeth a kiss as he went by. "Keep him straight, Mama."

She laughed. "I'm trying. Besides," she said punching me in the shoulder, "you've always said your heart belongs to only one woman."

She was right. There was only one that I could see myself with.

We spent the rest of the evening eating, drinking and reminiscing about the time we'd spent deployed. Debbie hooked up with one of the new guys who didn't know her history, and they left pretty early. Exhausted and a little drunk, I fell into bed sometime around three in the morning and woke to a house full of noise at seven.

I crawled down the stairs and saw Seth on his hands and knees with their oldest boy, Daniel, on his back while their daughter, Landry, led him across the den with their dog's leash around his neck. Their youngest child, John, was sitting in his highchair, giggling uncontrollably. He was only eighteen months old and not quite as daring as the others. He was more than content to sit and watch his older siblings torture their dad.

"Good morning," I heard MaryBeth say as she set a big plate of pancakes on the table. "Help yourself to some breakfast."

My stomach rolled as I thought about food combining with the eight or ten beers I'd chugged during the party. "How about just some coffee, please?" I made my way into the kitchen and zeroed in on the coffee pot.

"Help yourself," MaryBeth laughed. "Now that I've gotten mine, I'll share."

I poured a cup of coffee and left it black to get the full effect from it. As the steaming liquid burned my throat, I felt more human, and by the time I finished it, I was feeling pretty normal.

"Well, guys," I said, checking my watch. "I've got to get on the road. I had a blast and remember, you're welcome in Charlotte any time. I'll take you to a Panthers game or something."

Daniel jumped up and down. "Daddy! He's going to take us to a game!"

Seth patted his son on the head. "Slow your roll, Dan. That doesn't mean today."

Daniel dropped his head and hugged his dad tightly around his waist. "We might go, one day? Is that what you meant, Daddy?"

"Sure, little man. We'll all go see the Panthers play." Seth scooped John up and set him on his shoulders. "Uncle Ryder will make sure we get good tickets."

I laughed. "I can't promise they won't be in the nosebleed section but I'll see what I can do."

I gave everyone a hug, and as I pulled out of the driveway, I saw the entire Foust family waving enthusiastically in my mirror. I turned out onto the main road and made one last run through Fayetteville. I rolled downtown past the Airborne & Special Operations Museum where I'd attended some of the most emotional ceremonies in my life. I also rode around the famous Market House one last time before heading out of town. Despite its history of being a town full of pawn shops, strip clubs and cheap motels back in the Vietnam years, I'd found the town to be full of nice people who were very supportive of the military and when I was out in town, someone usually thanked me for my service. The military had been good to me, and I was excited to move forward in my civilian life with the skills I'd acquired.

As my bike and I rolled west to begin my new life, I let myself think of Jolene.

Chapter 3

Jolene

After imposing on my parents for a few weeks, it was finally time to move into my condo. Everyone pitched in to help, and I had my stored things moved in last. They'd finally arrived and were sitting in boxes lined up in my newly decorated living room. Olivia and I had spent the better part of a weekend picking out my new furniture, and it *had* looked neat and tidy until the delivery man dumped my personal belongings in the middle of the room. Diving in, I pulled the tape off the first box and the first thing I saw was a framed picture of myself with Giada at my first fashion week show. One of the photographers had sent it to her not caring who the 'girl' was in the picture but as soon as Giada saw it, she had it framed and gave it to me for my desk. Holding the picture in my hands, I backed over to the couch where I dropped down to perch on the edge. All of the emotions came welling up and just for a moment, I thought I caught a whiff of her favorite perfume. My head started buzzing, and I found myself swallowing back the urge to sob. I touched the cold glass in the frame as if trying to make contact with her, but I felt nothing but sadness and the ache of her loss. With a sigh, I placed the picture on a shelf by the window then began to unpack the rest of the box. My hair, which I'd left in its natural curly state, was getting in my way, so I piled it up into a messy bun.

I heard the intercom buzz, and I walked over to the phone.

"Yes?" I asked, expecting it to be the Chinese food I'd ordered earlier.

"Miss Anderson?" A deep male voice asked.

"Yes? Are you the delivery guy with my food? If you are, I'll buzz you up but if not, I'm not interested."

There was a pause then I heard a muffled, "Yeah."

My hunger overpowered my common sense, so I pushed the button to unlock the door and grabbed my wallet to pay for my food. My stomach growled its impatience as I hustled to the door. A moment later, after a very loud knock, I whipped open the door and found myself looking directly at a chiseled chest with broad arms crossed over it. My eyes traveled upward slowly until they locked on to the bluest eyes I'd ever seen, and they belonged to someone I knew well.

"Ryder…" I gasped.

"Hey, Jolene. You gonna invite me in?" He gave me a devilish grin causing me to stumble backwards pulling the door open along with me. He strolled in, his eyes taking in my condo while giving it an approving nod. Thankfully, he didn't notice my eyes scanning him from behind. His dark brown hair which had always been long and tousled was now close cropped. He was taller than I remembered and obviously had been working out, as evidenced by his muscles defined by his tight t-shirt. "Nice place you've got here. Making clothes must pay pretty well."

I nodded dumbly then realized what he'd said. "Making clothes? Ryder, I don't *make* clothes. I *design* them. Big difference," I said defensively.

He held up his hands and shrugged. "Sorry, I don't know how that works. What Uncle Sam didn't provide me with, I bought at Wallyworld." There was an awkward silence before he broke into a huge smile. "Where's my hug?"

That was the Ryder I knew. I ran to him and threw my arms around his neck. "I've missed my friend," I squealed as he wrapped his arms around me to lift me effortlessly from the ground.

"I missed you, too," he said softly in my ear. I was suddenly aware how tightly he was holding me with only my thin tank top and shorts covering me. He held me for a moment longer then set me back on the ground, his eyes taking in my appearance. I quickly grabbed a sweatshirt I had thrown on the couch and tried to act as casual as possible.

"It's good to see you, Ryder."

His eyes locked on mine for a moment, then he turned and started looking around my apartment again. "So, what brings you back? Mom said she was going to fill me in but I told her I'd rather see you in person and get the story. Everything okay? I thought you'd be over there forever."

"I…I lost someone very close to me," I answered with a sigh. "I had to get away from the memories. It was just too painful."

He studied my face. "Someone close to you…a boyfriend?"

Shaking my head, I scoffed. "No, it was my mentor, my friend, Giada Rinaldo. She died in a horrible plane crash and it really shook me." Walking over to the picture, I touched the frame gently. "It made me realize how fragile life really is."

He nodded. "I know exactly what you mean."

"Yeah, I guess you do." I gave him a sad smile. "Anyway, after her company was split apart and sold, I decided to come back here and start my own clothing design company." I stopped as I felt tears welling in my eyes. "It's really been rough."

He pulled me into a tight hug. "It had to be. I'm sorry you had to go through all that."

Suddenly, I realized he'd had to have gone through so much worse. "I'm so sorry. I didn't even consider what you've been through."

I felt him nod. "I loved them all like brothers and miss the hell out of them but the memories I have are what keep me sane. One day, you'll be able to remember the good times and not dwell on the bad."

The intercom buzzed causing me to jump back from his arms. Blushing furiously, I dashed to the intercom and heard a voice holler, "Tso Fu!" I hit the buzzer and within seconds, the delivery man knocked at the door. After grabbing my bag of Chicken Chow Mein and throwing some money at him, I turned almost bumping into Ryder, who was now standing right behind me.

"Well, I see you're ready to eat dinner so I'll roll. I'm sure I'll see you again soon, Jolene." He touched my cheek softly, and I impulsively stepped into it enjoying the comfort his touch brought to me.

"Are you sure you have to leave? I have plenty," I asked holding up the massive brown paper bag.

He smiled and gently stroked my chin. His blue eyes sparkled, and it struck me how gorgeous they were. "Enjoy. Really, I've gotta run. I'll be seeing you, though. I hope you get a great fortune cookie…" He backed to the door, opened it, and with a wave was gone. I dashed to the window and looked down to see him come out of the front door onto the street. A sleek black motorcycle was parked at the curb, and as he strapped on his helmet, he looked up at the window. I backed behind the curtain hoping I hadn't been spotted. I waited for the sound of the engine and heard him rev up as he pulled out onto the street. Risking a glance, I saw his bike rolling up to the next intersection where he got stopped by the light. As the light changed, he gave a nod back my way and then was gone.

I dropped onto the couch, my heart racing. "He saw me," I said out loud. "He freaking saw me." My face flushed again as I thought about how different Ryder was. "He's a kid," I said again out loud as if to convince myself but then I had to admit, he wasn't a kid anymore.

He was twenty-two and had served in the Army. He was a man, and a handsome, very muscular one at that. My starving stomach rumbled at me again so as I opened the container of Chow Mein and dug into my noodles, I thought about how radically things had changed in my life and actually felt a little scared by how quickly it had happened. When I'd finally eaten my fill, I thought about what Ryder had said and dug back into the bag for my fortune cookie. Cracking it open, I slid the tiny strip of paper out and read my fortune, 'The one you love is closer than you think'. For the first time, I really wished my fortune would come true.

The evening approached, and I felt so wired, I decided to take a walk downtown. Charlotte had always been my home, and I almost felt a need to reacquaint myself with the Queen City again. I grabbed my keys and my wallet and headed down to the street. The lights from the skyscrapers were beginning to illuminate the night sky, and since it was such a mild night, the sidewalks were crowded with Charlotteans going out to dinner in one of the trendy restaurants or to the Arts Center. I strolled along marveling at how laid back this big city really was compared to London. I stopped in front of a pub and decided to grab a glass of wine before heading back home. I'd just sat down at the end of the bar when I felt someone press against me. "Looking for a good time?" A deep voice growled in my ear.

Not wanting to cause a scene, I murmured, "Look asshole, I don't need company, or a good time for that matter." I kept my eyes straight ahead until I heard the laugh. I spun my head to the side to see Ryder leaning against the bar, and me. "Bloody Hell! What are you doing here?" I asked rolling my eyes. "I was just seconds from hitting you in the junk."

He backed up a step and laughed. "Let's not be too hasty! I'm here to meet my dad. He's working late and we're going to grab a bite to eat. And I believe your London is showing."

Shaking my head, I joined in the laughter. "Yeah, I lived there so long it rubbed off on me. So that's why my Chow Mein wasn't good enough for you…you had a date."

Ryder shrugged. "What can I say, he's hard to resist."

A hand squeezed my shoulder, and I turned to see Uncle Justin standing behind me with a big smile on his face. "Hey kids! What's going down?"

Ryder shook his head. "First of all Dad, nobody says that anymore. Secondly, Jolene was just seconds from hitting me in the junk."

Uncle Justin shrugged and set his briefcase on the bar. "Son, I haven't really had the chance to throw out the cool lingo. And…wha…? Junk?" He turned to me with his eyebrows raised. "What's he done now?"

When I just laughed and shrugged he shook his head and rolled his eyes. "Anyway, Jolene, you look radiant! Being back home seems to agree with you. You've got some color in your cheeks again. To be honest, you really had us worried when you first got back. I know it had to have been hard losing your friend like that."

"Thanks…I'm starting to feel a little more like myself," I answered softly.

The bartender came over, and they gave their orders. It gave me an opportunity to study Ryder without his eyes seemingly boring holes in my soul. He'd become very intense and yet when he'd smiled at me earlier, I'd seen the old Ryder under this new steely exterior.

Once again his deep blue eyes focused on me, and I quickly glanced away. "So, Jolene…will you join us or are you going to head back home?" Ryder asked as the overly eager waitress came to lead them to their table.

Watching her drooling over him with amusement, I checked my watch and pretended to stifle a yawn. "I think I'm going to head back. You guys enjoy your meal."

As I set my money on the bar for my wine, it was quickly picked up and stuffed back into my hand. "Let me buy your drink," Ryder said, his hand lingering on mine. I looked up and found him studying me closely. "Do you mind?"

I swallowed hard and shook my head no. "Thanks, Ryder," I said pulling my hand slowly from his. "I'll see you again soon, I'm sure."

"You can count on it," he said flashing a smile, before joining his dad at their table.

I left the pub and noticed immediately that the air had cooled, and as it hit my reddened cheeks, it felt refreshing. It also emphasized how flushed I'd become being around Ryder. I hadn't felt anything like this with him before, and I wondered to myself if it was just my heightened emotional state. As I climbed the stairs to my condo, I'd just about convinced myself it was just that. I was a wreck, and I needed to throw myself into my new business venture and steer clear of any man at this point.

The next morning, with a renewed focus, I made a call to a real estate agent my dad had suggested. She promised to get together some properties for me to consider as office/design space. We agreed to meet after lunch, so I unpacked a few more boxes and then dashed to her office, which wasn't far, only a few blocks. Susan Evans was one of the best in Charlotte and as a result, had carefully considered the distance from my home to a potential office space and had narrowed it down to three. We walked down the street, and she pointed up to one of the large bank buildings. "They have a space on the fourteenth floor that we're going to be looking at," she said as we entered the large glass doors. I was impressed that a doorman was stationed in the lobby as extra security. The elevator was a quiet and efficient one and within moments, we were deposited on the desired floor. The space was large and had an outside reception desk, which I made a mental check mark in the pro column for. There was a large room that could be used for showings as well as a huge office with a view of downtown. There was a conference room as well, and I immediately fell in love with it until I heard the noise through the wall.

"What is that?" I asked as the thumping continued.

She consulted her notes and gave me a small smile. "According to my paperwork, it's empty. They must be doing some reno work for a new tenant."

Assured the noise wasn't going to be an ongoing problem, I knew without going further, this was my place. "Susan, I think we have a winner." She was more than thrilled and mentioned that she'd shown me her favorite first, which I really appreciated. "Let's get your lease signed and you should be able to move in within the week."

We sat in the conference room and the landlord, who had offices on the second floor, came in to sign the papers with me. His name was Larry Masters, and he was about the same age as my grandpa, which gave me a good vibe. After all the documents were signed, and I'd paid my deposits, he handed me a key ring with the office keys on it. "I hope you'll be very happy here," he said patting me on the back then shaking my hand. "If you need anything at all, please don't hesitate to call me."

I left the office excited but also a bit nervous about setting everything up by myself. However, I took a deep breath and headed back home to start calling all the necessary people to get things in motion. By the time I got all of my phone calls made it was dark, so I stepped out onto my balcony cradling a glass of wine and listened to the hum of the city beneath me. I was so lost in my thoughts that I didn't hear my phone ring until it chimed signaling a voicemail. It was my mom, and I called her back right away.

"Hey, Sweet Pea," she said cheerfully. "How are you? I feel like I haven't talked to you in days."

"I'm sorry, Mom. I'm good. I've just been super busy. I leased an office today and I should be able to move in by the end of the week."

"Oh, Jolene, that's wonderful. I was hoping you'd find something pretty quickly so you can get back to work and keep your mind off of..." Her words trailed off, and I knew what she'd been about to say.

"You're right, Mom. I do need something to occupy my mind. This will be good for me."

I heard a muffled voice in the background and then her reply. "Your sister doesn't need you hanging around, Ethan. She's got enough on her plate as it is."

"Mom, tell Ethan that I'll need a strong pair of arms when I get ready to set up my office. Ask him if he'll keep this Saturday free."

She covered the phone to relay the message then said, "He'll be ready when you call."

"Thanks for checking on me, and y'all have a great evening."

I heard a squeal from my mom. "You just said 'y'all'! It's not completely gone out of you!" She was so excited I hadn't lost my Southern charm.

Laughing, I said, "Mom, I was born and raised here. Do you think I've changed that much?"

She joined in the laughter. "You're right. I'm just thrilled that you still have that in you. I'm going to let you go but please don't forget to call Ethan. He wants so badly to spend time with you."

"I will. Oh! By the way, guess who showed up at my door the other night?"

There was a brief silence then, "Um, I'm guessing Ryder?" The guilty tone let me know she was the one who'd sent him my way. "How did he know how to find you?"

I laughed. "Mom, you're so transparent. I had a feeling you told him where I was living."

She tsked at me. "Really, Jolene. I'm still your mother and what you just said implies that I'm lying. Did you consider that your aunt Callie may have told him?"

"Aunt Callie doesn't know where I live, Mom."

Another pause. "Oh, well then I may have mentioned it to Ryder when he stopped by to see us the other day. He's such a handsome young man, isn't he?"

I had to admit he really was. "Yeah, he's changed a lot. I enjoyed seeing him," I said picturing Ryder standing at my door gazing down at me with those deep blue eyes.

"Jolene?"

"Huh?" I realized she asked me a question and had not a clue what it was. Trying to bluff I said, "I'm sorry the television is on. What did you say?"

"I asked if you'd heard from Tyler. He's trying to get in touch with you."

My biological dad, Tyler and I had spoken right before I left London, and I knew he was supposed to be traveling out of the country with his wife and their kids on a mission trip for his church. The fact he was trying to reach me worried me a little. "I'll try to call him. Thanks for telling me. He probably left me a voicemail but I've been so busy, I haven't had time to listen to them."

My mom said, "Well, let me know what's going on when you talk to him, okay?" Despite the fact that he fled when he found out my mom was pregnant with me, they'd moved past all the hard feelings for my sake. It had been awkward at first but over time, everyone became comfortable with the situation. He understood that Jay was my dad and never tried to take that role. My dad had always been prepared to allow Tyler back into my life, if and when he deserved to be, and after years of sobriety it happened. After the initial shock of finding out that the man I knew as Mr. Tyler was, in fact, my real father, I found that I held no animosity toward him but instead felt sympathy. He explained that he'd been immature and stupid when he'd walked out on my mom and years later, when he tried to come back into our lives, he'd almost died as a result. A drunk driving accident almost took him out but it was also the wakeup call he'd needed to realize he wasn't ready to be a dad and taking me away from my mom wasn't going to benefit me. He'd abandoned his selfish ways and, with the help of his wife, Cailynn, left town so they could start a new life together. I'd flown out to visit him a couple of times when their kids, Eva and Will, were little and we'd kept in touch by video chat while I was in England as often as I could work it into my busy schedule.

I told my mom goodnight and checked my voicemails. I found thirty-nine waiting for me to listen to and as I went through each one, I jotted down whether they were important or headed straight for delete. I had one message from Lucinda who said she was just checking in and a few from colleagues from the design house in London offering their support. One was very urgent. The caller, a Nigerian prince, needed me to call him back as soon as possible because he was going to pay off all of my debts! As tempting as that was, I deleted it without calling him back and made sure to block that number so I wouldn't hear from him again. Finally, I got to the message from Tyler.

"Hey, I've been trying to reach you. Call me when you get a minute, okay? Love you!"

I called him back, and he answered on the first ring.

"Boy, you sure know how to worry a guy!" He exclaimed. "You usually call me back right away."

"I know. I've been swamped since I got back and when Mom told me you'd called, I checked my messages right away. I'm sorry."

"Sweetie, it's okay. I just worry about my kids," he laughed. "So, how are things going since you got back?"

I dropped onto my couch and curled up. "I'm doing better. It's going to take some adjusting but I'll be okay. It just hurts. Giada was so good to me."

There was a silence then he said softly, "You were supposed to go on the trip with her, weren't you? Your mom said you got sick and had to cancel. I'm really sorry about your friend, but I'm so thankful that you weren't on that plane."

I blinked back tears and took a deep breath. "Yeah, I should have been with her."

"No, no, you shouldn't have. It wasn't your destiny, Jolene. God has a design for all of our lives..."

We were both silent for a moment and in that span of time, I realized that he wasn't just talking about me or my trip. He was talking about himself, my mom, my dad, everything. All of our lives had changed because of decisions people had made in their lives, whether good ones or bad ones. Tyler had a rough life and if my mom and I had been in his life during that time, we would have suffered for it. Because he chose to leave, my mom found the love of her life who took me as his own child, giving me his name.

"I understand what you're saying, but it still hurts," I sighed.

"I know it's hard but just know you've got a family that loves you and is here for you.   We're going to try to plan a family trip out there to see you as soon as we can."

"That's great! Keep me informed on a date and I'll be sure to clear my calendar. Is everyone doing okay?"

"We sure are. I just finished my training and will be an ordained minister as soon as I get back to the states. The kids are enjoying learning the new culture but I know they're ready to go home. It should only be another couple of months and we'll be finished with the school." I heard a voice in the background and he paused. "Hold on, Jolene." I could hear muffled talking and then he was back. "Sorry, it looks like they need me for a plumbing issue. I've gotta go."

"That's okay, just tell everyone that I said hi and that I love them!" With a quick goodbye, he was gone.

I climbed in my pajamas and slid into bed.   I picked up my Kindle but couldn't concentrate. Instead, I replayed the phone call in my head and smiled. I did have a wonderful family, and I was surrounded by love. I vowed to honor Giada's memory by living each day to the fullest and letting everyone who I cared about know exactly how I felt. I started feeling really drowsy, so I set my Kindle on the nightstand, curled up into a ball and fell fast asleep.

Chapter 4

Ryder

I climbed from my motorcycle and looked up at the glass monster in front of me. Skyscrapers really weren't my style but because my dad had helped design the building and had become friends with the owner, I got a really great deal on some office space. My plan was to open a security company with the money I'd diligently saved while serving in the Army. While my buddies were spending their pay on fast cars so they could impress women, I'd bought a used motorcycle and stayed clear of the women trolling in the bars. I had my training to back me up and once I'd secured the necessary licenses, I was ready to get started. I'd even decided on a name for my business, Solitaire Security. Stepping around a moving truck parked in the loading zone, I found my way into the reception area. The doorman, Drake Hoskins, who I'd met when I came in to sign the lease, greeted me and signed me in. The office had already been up fitted per my dad's instructions, and it was move-in ready. The first thing on my agenda was to hire some employees and get to work. As I stepped off the elevator, I noticed several movers sliding a mahogany wardrobe through the door of the office next to mine. They had the furniture wedged in so, feeling neighborly, I helped them lift it all the way through without scratching it. They thanked me profusely and I assured them it was not a big deal, then I headed into my office. My dad had definitely known what I needed for my particular line of work and worked that into the design of my office. I had a conference room for clients, a room for displaying and demonstrating the various security devices, a records room that was safeguarded for keeping my client's information confidential and a luxurious office for myself. He'd spent my money well. I brewed some coffee and was about to pour a cup for myself when I heard the outer door open.

"Come in, I'll be out in a sec," I hollered out as I grabbed the cup and headed to the outer office. "Good morn—," I stopped when I saw a massive man trying to squeeze himself into one of the reception chairs. He straightened as I walked in and towered over me, surpassing me by at least six inches in height. He smiled, and I knew right away, he was one of those people who look intimidating but are just teddy bears at heart. "Good morning." I glanced at my appointment I had saved on my phone. "Mr. Yancy? I'm Ryder Brisson."

He extended a huge hand that enveloped mine. With a deep, booming voice, he said, "Hi, I'm Darryl." I shook his hand firmly and indicated for him to follow me to the conference room.

"So, tell me, did you ever play pro football?" I asked as I motioned for him to take a seat.

He laughed a deep rumbling laugh. "Nah, just some college ball. I got hurt in my senior year so I didn't go pro."

"Man, that sucks," I said as I offered him a cup of coffee.

He shook his head no and said with a smile, "Thanks but I'm trying to watch the weight."

I took in his biceps and broad chest. "Darryl, I think you have what it takes to work security, that's obvious. Now, let's look at your resume." Quickly scanning through, it was obvious that he had loads of experience as well. "So, you did bodyguard work for some of the pro football players, I see. Sounds like a pretty good deal."

He nodded. "It was, but I hate to say it, I couldn't deal with the egos. Money goes to some people's heads and that's all I'm gonna say about that."

Smiling, I had to agree. Celebrities could be the best clients or your worst nightmares. My dad had dealt with some of that when he was designing buildings for some of the local race drivers. One client had been a dream, approving every suggestion my dad had given him without argument but then when he was referred to the client's friend, it was another story. That client had demanded final approval on every last detail after which my dad vowed to never do work for that type of client again.

"Well, Darryl," I said standing while extending my hand. "Welcome aboard. Come in Monday and we'll try to put you to work." As we shook hands, he gave me a huge smile.

"Thank you so much for the opportunity, Mr. Brisson."

"Call me Ryder," I said returning the smile.

I had my first employee and now I needed to work on getting some clients. I'd done security work in the military protecting very high ranking officers but that didn't always translate to the real world. Opening my laptop, I started googling some local celebs and sent out some emails offering my services. What I needed foremost was one big client to entice others to follow suit. A few hours later, I grabbed my phone, locked up the office, stepped around the movers who were halfway blocking the hallway with a leather couch, and headed down in the elevator.

My phone rang while I was listening to the elevator's version of Lady Gaga's 'Bad Romance'. It was a number I didn't recognize.

"Solitaire Security, Ryder Brisson speaking."

"Yes, Mr. Brisson, this is Kimberly Rafe. I'm the personal assistant to Ryanne Charles. We received your email and it came at a most opportune time. Ms. Charles has just relieved her previous security firm of their duties and we were very impressed by your resume."

Ryanne Charles was a very popular model/actress who had recently stepped away from Hollywood to come back to her Southern roots and settle down. She was one of the first names who popped up on my search of local celebs. She was so popular, plus she had married Rusty MacNeil, who was the hottest driver in the racing series.

"Well, thank you, Ms. Rafe. I can assure you it's accurate and you are more than welcome to check my references."

She laughed. "Oh we've already done that. Ms. Charles is very thorough."

"So, do you want to set up a meeting? I'll be glad to meet at her convenience."

She hesitated then said, "Could you hold just a moment?" A moment later she returned. "Mr. Brisson, she would like you to come to her home tomorrow morning, if that works for you."

I scrolled through my calendar quickly and saw I was free until noon when I was expecting another job applicant. "I can meet her around ten if that's good."

"Yes, that's perfect. Let me give you the address."

By now I was in the lobby so I begged a piece of paper from Drake and jotted down the information. I recognized the address as being on Lake Norman where many of the drivers had homes.

"Got it! I'll be there at ten. Tell Ms. Charles I really appreciate the opportunity."

"I will. Just ring the intercom at the gate when you arrive and someone will let you in. See you tomorrow."

"Goodbye." I hung up the phone and smiled. I had a fish on the hook, now I just needed to reel it in.

The next morning, wearing a black pair of dress slacks and a charcoal grey button-up, I pulled up to the gate promptly at ten in my rented black Expedition. I definitely needed to invest in a car and after driving this one I was already a fan. After pressing the call button, it was only a moment before I heard a voice I recognized as Ms. Rafe's.

I glanced up and saw the video camera had rotated to face me. I gave a little wave and the gate opened. Making a mental note to mention they really hadn't identified me before allowing me access, I realized that this had to be the way things had been done by the previous security company. If the job went to me then it was going to be run a lot tighter. Driving up the long driveway, I finally saw the front of their massive home. Carefully manicured lawns flanked the driveway leading to a grand entry with wrought iron railings leading to two giant wooden doors. As I parked, the wooden door opened and an attractive blonde woman, who looked to be in her forties, made her way to my truck. I grabbed my briefcase and met her at the curb.

"Mr. Brisson, I'm Kimberly Rafe. We spoke on the phone."

"Nice to meet you, Ms. Rafe," I said holding out my hand which she took, giving it a firm shake.

"Please, call me Kimberly. Ms. Charles is in the conservatory. I'll take you there." I followed her up the stairs, through the impressive doors and into a foyer that was three stories tall, featuring a spiral staircase that wound all the way to the top. Expensive throw rugs dotted the pristine marble floors and arrangements of fresh flowers were set on almost every piece of furniture, all which appeared to be rare antiques.

We passed the housekeeper who was dusting a portrait of Ms. Charles, and I stopped for a moment to admire it. I thought the artist had done a really amazing job of capturing her beauty until we stepped into the conservatory and I saw her in person. She was standing by the French doors, her back to me, but when she heard us enter the room she turned and I was struck by how perfect her features were. Her blonde hair was tied with a ribbon, and it was draped across her shoulder. She had very little makeup on from what I could see, just pure, natural beauty.

"Mr. Brisson, this is Ryanne Charles," Kimberly said as an introduction.

Ms. Charles glided across the space between us and I could see a model's grace in her walk. "Mr. Brisson, it's so nice to meet you."

I felt a little star struck but quickly recovered. "Please, call me Ryder."

"Ryder. I like that." She indicated to a leather wingback chair and I took a seat. "So, Ryder, please tell me where to start."

Opening my briefcase, I took out my checklist that I'd brought along with my contract. "I have a few questions to help me determine what I can offer you and then if you have any questions or concerns, I'll be glad to address them." When she nodded, I continued, "First, is the security for just yourself or are there multiple clients?"

She answered immediately. "This is for myself and my two year old, Gage. My husband, Rusty, has his own security and I didn't like the way they handled me, which is why they've been fired."

Nodding, I made a note on my sheet and moved to the next question. "Is this a full-time security detail or just on an event basis?"

She hesitated then shrugged. "I think it's probably best as a full-time basis. I've had some issues with some obsessed fans. I still do some modeling on occasion but it's mostly local so I don't have to leave Gage too long. Rusty is out of town a lot and I don't like dragging Gage from place to place for races. We do some of the close ones like Charlotte and Richmond but I'm not going to Texas or Las Vegas just to sit in the motor home while the race is going on. It isn't fair to Gage to have him sleeping in a different place every night for weeks at a time. Rusty tries to fly home when he can and spend time with us here."

"So, who handles your home security?" I asked looking up.

She hesitated. "Right now? Nobody. We have our alarm hooked up to a security monitoring company but no one hands on." She smiled sheepishly. "I realized after Kimberly buzzed you right in that we'd made a mistake but you were already on the property. We really need someone to come in to set us up with a home security plan that we can feel safe with."

I jotted a couple of things down then gave her a smile. "Ms. Charles, I really believe I can help you. I'm just starting out in the civilian world but have been doing security details for some of the top ranking officers in the Army. I'm from the area so I'm familiar with many locations already and would have no trouble surveying places that you plan to be ahead of time. I just hired an employee, Darryl Yancy, who has done security for several professional football players and between the two of us, I believe we can do the job. I'm also going to be hiring more security officers within the next day or so. We can offer you home security and personal security, as much or as little as you wish."

She gave a sigh of relief. "Thank you so much. Rusty really wasn't happy when I fired his guys but I feel you're more in tune with the type of lifestyle I lead. When can you start?"

Pulling the contract from my briefcase, I smiled and said, "As soon as we sign these papers, I'm all yours!"

When I arrived back at my office, my next applicant was waiting in the lobby. Drake had been entertaining him until I got back so we rode up to the office together. His name was Joey Andrews, and he was former military like myself. Tall, lean and blonde, he had the look of a surfer rather than a bodyguard, but I was willing to give him a chance. We sat in the conference room as I ran through the usual questions and was very impressed by his experience and knowledge. "So, you've done some embassy security. How was that?

"Very interesting, sir. Luckily, I wasn't in a particularly dangerous area but dealing with diplomats was pretty scary at times."

I laughed. "Been there myself! And, Joey, you don't have to address me as 'sir'. Ryder is fine."

He smiled. "Sure thing."

"So, where are you from originally?" I asked as I took notes.

"Originally, Jacksonville, Florida. I grew up on the beach."

I laughed. "Yeah, looking at you, I could tell."

He grinned. "When I joined the Army, they sent me to Kansas. I was miserable being so far from the ocean. I was stoked when I got sent to Bragg and could hit the ocean on the weekends again."

"You were at Bragg? So was I!" We started comparing notes and found we had several friends in common. "Small world, huh?" I said shaking my head. I liked Joey and knew he'd be a great fit for the company. Having already done a background check, the only thing left to do was offer him the job which he readily accepted. I had a crew. I had a client. Things were going exactly the way I'd planned.

Chapter 5

Jolene

The wardrobe looked amazing in the corner of my new showroom and I ran my hand along the polished wood feeling the intricate carvings under my fingers. It had been my paternal grandmother's and when she'd passed away, it had been put in storage. When they were settling her estate, Tyler asked me if I'd like to have it. Sentimentality being my strong suit, I readily accepted. It had gone into my bedroom at my parent's home and now, with Ethan's help, it was safely tucked in my office. It was perfect for holding fabric and samples to display for the clients.

Fingers crossed, today, I was going to land what would be a lucrative contract with one of the largest boutiques in Charlotte. They wanted exclusive rights to some of my previous designs and also wanted some new ones created just for them. Checking my watch, I noticed it was just about time for the CEO to arrive. I heard a noise outside the door, so I opened it to welcome my guest. Instead, I found a huge man outside my door headed into the office next door. He turned and gave me a nod and a smile as he passed. Quickly, I backed into my office and shut the door. I grabbed the phone and dialed the lobby.

"Drake? This is Jolene Anderson. Could you tell me what kind of business is in the office next door to me?"

"Yes, ma'am. It's a private security company. Is there a problem?" He asked.

"No, I'm sorry to bother you. I just saw someone going in and wondered. Thank you and have a nice day." I hung up the phone and leaned against my desk. Private security. The guy going in the office definitely fit the stereotype for a bodyguard. What could it hurt to have a security company next door? It would certainly make me feel safer when I had to work late.

"Hello?" I heard a voice call out from the outer office. "Ms. Anderson?"

"Coming!" I replied. I checked myself in the mirror, then dashed out to meet Maxine Abernathy, CEO of Maxine's Closet. She was a woman of about fifty, impeccably dressed with her gray hair swept into a twist.

"Ms. Abernathy! So happy to meet you in person finally!" We'd spoken several times on the phone since my return, and I was thrilled to be working with her.

"Please, honey, call me Maxine," she said giving my hand a squeeze. "I feel like I know you already, Ms. Anderson."

"Jolene. Please call me Jolene." I escorted her into my conference room and offered her a cup of coffee. I'd already sketched some things for her to look at so she sat with my tattered design pad flipping through the pages. She loved them and had only minor changes which I was able to sketch for her and obtain her approval on right away.

"Now, for the advertising campaign, I want a model people will recognize. Do you have anyone we can use?" She asked.

"To be honest, I haven't contracted any models yet but I have a few in mind that are local. I can get in contact with them and if they're interested pass the information on to you for final approval," I said as I jotted some notes on the designs.

She smiled and stood to leave. "I trust your judgment. Your work is impeccable and I'm excited to be working with you. I believe this partnership will be a huge benefit to the both of us."

I walked her to the elevator and was coming back to the office when I ran into my neighbor, the giant, again. "Good afternoon, ma'am," he rumbled.

"Hi," I said feeling dwarfed by his stature. "Apparently, you're my new neighbor. I'm Jolene Anderson." I held out my hand which was enveloped by his. "So, you own a security business?"

He laughed a deep belly laugh. "My name's Darryl Yancy. Nice to meet you. As for the business, I just work there. As a matter of fact, I just got my first assignment."

I raised my brows and gave him a grin. "Someone famous? Anybody I'd know?"

His blue eyes twinkled and again he laughed making me chuckle as well. "Actually, it's a model who lives here in Charlotte. I can't say any more than that for privacy reasons but it's a really great gig."

Pouting, I shrugged my shoulders. "I understand. It couldn't hurt to ask."

"So what do you do, Ms. Anderson?"

"Coincidentally, I'm a fashion designer. I've just opened my own design company and I just got my first client. I guess we're both rookies."

Our conversation was interrupted by his phone. "Yancy." He listened for a moment. "Yes, I was just heading to her house now. I have the address and will call when I get everything set up."

I waved goodbye to give him some privacy and he held up his hand to wave goodbye then turned to get on the elevator. The last thing I heard as the doors were closing was, "Yes sir, I will take good care of Ms. Charles."

A light bulb went off in my head. Ryanne Charles. I ran into my office to Google her and sure enough, after a little digging, I found a website that said she was now living at Lake Norman with her husband and son. The images of her online were spectacular and ideal for the designs I was going to be doing. I jotted down her agency's phone number and made a note to call to see if she was available.

"Yo! Jolene!" The door of my office opened slowly and Olivia popped her head in. "Your cheap labor is here."

"Liv, you're hardly that. Plus, by being my assistant, you'll get lots of perks." I rocked back in my chair.

She grinned. "Speaking of perks, I just saw a totally hot guy going into the office next door."

I laughed. "Yeah, I saw that guy…tall, bald and totally hot!"."

She frowned. "No, the guy I saw was tall, *blonde* and totally hot."

"Well, then there must be more than one guy over there," I said with a shrug. "Now, back to your *real* perks. Just think, you'll get samples of all the latest designs, especially since we're going to be working with Maxine's Closet!"

A huge smile spread across her face. "You got the account? Congrats! That's a big deal! You know? I think I'm really gonna like being your assistant. What do you need me to do first?"

I returned the smile and handed her a phone number. "Your first assignment…get me Ryanne Charles."

A few hours later, I was putting the finishing touches on a cute mini-dress design when Olivia came bouncing into the office. "Ms. Charles will meet with you tomorrow morning at ten. How's that for service?"

My mouth dropped open. "How'd you manage that?" I gasped.

She grinned and shrugged as she perched on the corner of my desk examining her nails. "It seems that you are more famous than you think, big sister. I just threw your name around with some of the people who might know her and within no time, I had her personal phone number. I called and spoke to her assistant and again, as soon as I said your name, she put me right through to Ryanne Charles herself. It didn't take much to convince her to come talk to you, especially when I told her you were working with Maxine's Closet on a campaign."

I continued to stare at her. "She knew who I was? I mean, that's crazy!"

Olivia shook her head. "Really? Are you serious? You are one of the hottest designers in the world! Of course she'd know who you were! Duh!"

I was floored. Ryanne Charles? I'd been star struck by some of the many celebrities whom Giada had as clients but Ryanne was my all-time favorite. She'd been discovered as a teenager and had quickly become one of the highest paid models in the business. Her modeling career led to a part in a movie where she really showed her talent. She became American's sweetheart, and the world was captivated when she suddenly turned up on the arm of bad-boy race driver Rusty MacNeil. They became an item and within a year were engaged, which led to a million dollar wedding in Hilton Head, South Carolina.

When their baby was born a year later, the world was introduced to Gage Martin McNeil. Then came an announcement that shocked Ryanne's fans. She'd decided to give up her lucrative career in acting to be a full-time mom. I'd heard rumors that she had gotten a little stir crazy at home and was interested in taking on some work close to home. This was a perfect opportunity to get her back into the modeling world, even if it was just part-time.

Olivia's fingers tapping on the desk refocused my attention on what she was saying. "Do you realize how great this would be? I'm sure she has tons of model friends who would jump at the chance to work with you."

Olivia was right. I actually got a little nervous thinking about her coming to my office. I'd always had Giada by my side when working with my designs, and now I was going at it all alone.

As a team, Olivia and I spent the rest of the morning organizing my office and setting up the display room. Olivia had a great sense of décor and had no trouble putting all of my things in their proper place. Seeing it was way past quitting time, I grabbed my things from my desk as she came in and plopped down in the chair across from me.

"You up for a glass of wine tonight?" She asked with a grin.

I sighed. "Honestly? Not really. I need to head home and get my things organized for tomorrow. I'm sorry."

She shrugged and nodded. "Okay, I understand. I may just head to the little bar down the street for a quick one."

As she walked out the door, I yelled after her, "Be careful!"

"I always am!" She threw back over her shoulder before pulling the door closed.

Rubbing my neck, I stretched it from side to side. I was tired but I knew this was not a night to go home and veg on the couch. I had a lot of work to do before my meeting tomorrow morning. Grabbing my bag, I walked out, locking the door firmly behind me.

"Well, well, what have we here?" I jumped when I heard the voice behind me. Immediately, I had my pepper spray in my hand and spun to find myself face to face with Ryder.

"What are you doing here? Spying on me?" I asked frowning.

His eyebrows shot up as he held out his hands in surrender. "You got me!" He said laughing. "Seriously, I was just coming to do some last minute paperwork." He pointed to the office next door that now had "Solitaire Security" in bold letters on it.

My mouth fell open. "You're with the guys next door?"

He grinned and nodded. "Yep, it's my company. Looks like you're stuck with me as a neighbor." He pulled out his keys and walked to the door. "Would you like a tour? It's free."

I looked at my watch and saw it was getting late but my curiosity was piqued, so I strolled to the door. "Who did your decorating?"

He pushed open the door and flipped on the light. "Me," he said throwing his keys on the side table.

The office was amazing. A plump dark leather couch filled the waiting area along with two equally impressive side chairs. A flat screen television was mounted on the wall and a well-stocked fish tank flanked the other wall. I walked over to the tank and tapped on the glass. I could see Ryder's reflection in the glass as he came up behind me.

"Pretty impressive, huh?" He asked as he dropped some flakes into the water. "Fish are pretty soothing and in my line of work, that's the kind of atmosphere we want." He strolled over and pushed open a door to an inner office. He placed his hand on the small of my back. "Come see where I hang out," he said with a grin.

I let him lead me to a roomy office fit for an executive, complete with a large wooden desk with a leather desk chair and matching leather couch. Shelves filled with books about law and self-defense lined the walls. I ran my fingers along the spines of the books and had to admit, I was pretty impressed with the subject matter. A modern flat screen computer perched on the corner of his desk along with a few manila folders stacked in a 'To Be Filed' tray. He had two file cabinets in the back corner along with several boxes that apparently had yet to be unpacked.

I spun, leaned against the desk, and gave him a big smile. "Very nice, Mr. Brisson. I like what I see."

Again his eyebrows shot up. With a smile framed by adorable dimples, he said, "Why, thank you. As a matter of fact, so do I."

I felt a flush creep across my cheeks. "Ahem, the office, Ryder...the office."

He stepped closer, close enough I could feel the heat from his body. "I really missed you, Jolene. More than you know." He brushed my cheek with his fingertips.

My breathing quickened, and I realized my palms were sweating. "Um, I missed you too, Ryder," I said as calmly as possible. "Just like I missed Carter and Ethan."

He sighed and took a step back.

I instantly regretted what I'd said. Unfortunately, I could feel this was going in a direction I didn't want it to go. I scrambled. "No, of course not. What I mean is, you've been...I've..."

My phone rang, mercifully interrupting my foolish stammering. Holding up my finger, I answered Olivia's call. "Hello?"

I could barely hear her for the loud music in the background. "Hey Jo! Whatcha doin?"

I looked up to find Ryder's eyes locked on me. "Um, just talking to Ryder. Did you know his office is right next door to ours?"

There was a pause. "No way! How convenient is that…I mean, how cool!" She shouted.

"Very…so what's up?"

She giggled loudly. "Oh, well I met someone here at the bar and he's super hot. The only thing is, he has a friend and I was hoping you'd come down and hang out with us for a drink…just one, I promise."

Closing my eyes, I took a deep breath. "Crikey, Olivia, I don't want to be set up with some guy just to make things easier for you." Out of the corner of my eye, I saw Ryder shuffling some papers on his desk. "I mean, I can come have one drink with you but I'm not being pawned off on his friend, capiche?"

"Did you just go all British/Italian on me?" She said laughing. "Look, it's a fun place, you need to unwind a little. Come to the bar and have a drink. You deserve it."

I sighed. There was no arguing with her. "Okay, okay. Just one. I'll be there in a few minutes."

Throwing my phone into my purse, I turned to find Ryder watching me intently as he sat perched on the corner of his desk. "Hot date?" He asked with a frown.

I scoffed. "Hardly. Olivia's met someone and wants me to be her wingman…or wingwoman…whatever. I really just wanted to go home and climb into a bath full of bubbles."

"Hmm," he said with a devilish grin. "Sounds like a perfect night."

"Yeah," I said, trying to ignore his implications but feeling my face flush. "Well *you* can go home. Unfortunately, it looks like *I'm* going to be stuck for at least a little while longer."

He stood and gently took me by the elbow. "Well, you'd better not keep him…I mean, them, waiting. I'll walk you down." After he locked up, we walked to the elevator. His phone rang as we climbed on, and he checked the caller then answered. "Brisson."

I could only hear his end of the conversation but it sounded from my perspective that he was lining up his client for the next day.

"Yes, ma'am. I'll be there at around 8:30 in the morning to go over the schedule and then either Mr. Yancy or myself, will be escorting you for the day."

I watched the floor numbers flash on the display as we descended to the lobby. I didn't like listening in on a business call, especially one involving someone's security. "Yes, ma'am. I have the gate code and will let myself in. See you then."

He ended the call and leaned back against the back wall of the elevator. "So, when are you going to let me take you to dinner?" He asked.

I turned and looked at him with surprise. "Wha--?" I spluttered.

"Dinner, you...me...when?" He grinned as he opened the calendar on his phone. "I'm free pretty much any time, especially for you."

Just then the elevator door opened. I stood there staring at him until he took me by the arm and led me out before the doors closed and I went back up again. "Just say the word and I'm yours," he whispered as we walked across the deserted lobby. I was about to answer when he noticed a different doorman manning the front desk. Ryder immediately approached him and glancing at his name tag said, "Kris, is it? I'm Ryder Brisson. I own Solitaire Security. Is this your usual shift?"

I noticed that 'Kris' backed a couple of steps back. "Y...yes, sir. I'm Kris Taylor. I've been on this shift for about two months now. Most people don't see me because by the time I come on duty they're gone for the day."

Ryder nodded slowly and held out his hand to shake his. "Okay, good to know. I work all kinds of odd hours so I like to know who's keeping an eye on the people going in and out of here. Plus," he said indicating toward me. "There are ladies who work in the building and their safety is my number one priority."

Kris swallowed hard as he returned the shake. "Yes, sir. I take my job very seriously."

We left him standing at the desk and went out the doors into the mild evening air. As soon as the doors closed behind us, I giggled. "Did you have to scare the poor man to death?"

Ryder's eyes narrowed. "Jolene, security is not a laughing matter. In my firm, I'm one hundred percent responsible for my clients and I take that very seriously. A doorman may just be a doorman to you but he's also a line of defense against someone who wants to get in the building to do mischief."

I stopped and stared. "Ryder…when did you become an old man? Mischief? Seriously?"

His serious expression relaxed, and he gave me a grin. "Sorry, sometimes my military shows. I learned to be very suspicious of even the most innocent looking passerby. Afghanistan was a very sobering learning experience."

We strolled in silence to the bar and once we reached the door, he stopped. "Please promise me you and Olivia will be careful. I feel weird leaving you with some guys she just met."

I pulled my pepper spray from my bag and tucked it into my hand. "I'm prepared. Let him get too close and he'll be crying for days."

Ryder smiled. "That's my girl. Look, seriously, if you get in a bind, just text me. I'll come running."

Placing my hand on his arm, I gave it a squeeze. "You got it! Thanks for everything." Without thinking, I kissed his cheek and walked into the bar.

Chapter 6

Ryder

Touching my cheek where she'd just kissed me, I watched the door close behind her and felt so conflicted. "Meeting some guy in a bar," I mumbled under my breath. "What the hell is Olivia thinking?" I started to walk away, but something made me turn back. I slipped in the door and blended in with the crowd. I might as well keep an eye on her since I was already here. Olivia was waving at her from the bar, and I could see two men sitting on either side of her. The men were dressed in business suits and from the array of empty glasses on the bar, they'd been there a while. Jolene walked up, gave her sister a hug and was quickly introduced to their companions. One of the men, a tall blonde, had his arm slung over Olivia's shoulders, so I assumed the man with the black hair was for Jolene. They scooted down to open up a barstool for Jolene, and I saw her guy throw up his hand to the bartender to order her a drink. In my line of work, observing body language is very important and watching the clown trying to work his mojo on her was making me sick. He 'accidentally' brushed her thigh with his hand and then patted it firmly to apologize for the accident. No accident. I could see she was uncomfortable, closing herself off to him, but he wasn't getting the hint. My blood began to boil as I watched the scene play out in front of me.

"Well, hello there!" I heard a woman say as her hand brushed across my ass. "All alone and looking for some company?"

I turned to see a girl about my age, who was wearing way too much makeup, pressing her chest against me while flashing a mile of leg in the process. Looking her up and down, I knew this was NOT going to happen. "Look, I'm waiting for someone. If you're looking for a date, try somewhere else."

She pouted but refused to back away. She ran a long red nail over my cheek. "You know, you just need to relax. I'm a sure thing. I had my eye on you the instant you walked in." She cupped my butt and gave it a squeeze.

I was just about to say something rude when suddenly, Jolene came up beside me and wrapped her arm around my waist. "Look, he said he's not interested and he means it. He told you he was waiting for someone and now I'm here, so back off, hussy!"

Biting my lip to keep from laughing, I watched as the 'hussy' *had she really called her that*? skulked away into the shadows. Jolene remained standing there with her finger still in the poking position so I wrapped my hand around hers then brought it to my lips. "Thank you for saving me," I murmured. "I hope I didn't interrupt your evening."

Her brilliant blue eyes were looking up at me. "Nah, I'd just finished my obligatory drink and saw you'd stuck around. That's when I saw the vulture come circling and figured you might need my help. Why are you still here, anyway?" She asked slowly withdrawing her hand from mine.

"Well, to tell you the truth, I'd come in here expecting to save you, but here we are. If designing clothes doesn't pay the bills, I can find you a position in my security firm. By the way...hussy?"

She laughed. "Sorry, that's what Lucinda used to say to the hoochies when we were out clubbing. And as far as the job goes, I'll keep that in mind." She looked up to see Olivia signaling that a cab was waiting. When Olivia saw me, her eyebrows shot up and I saw a trace of a smile. Jolene pressed herself against me and with a suggestive tone in her voice said, "G'night, Ryder. I'll see you around." She ran her nail down my cheek and then gave it a pinch. "Try to stay out of trouble."

Swallowing hard, I managed to say, "I'm right behind you," as I rushed to open the door for the two of them. "You girls be safe."

Olivia grinned at me. "Goodnight, Ryder."

I stood on the sidewalk watching as they got in their cab and drove out of sight. I walked the two blocks back to the building where I'd parked the SUV and then drove home, my mind focused on that blue-eyed enigma that was Jolene.

The next morning, bright and early, I went for my morning jog, grabbed some coffee then headed to the office. Darryl and Joey were already there. We'd agreed to tone down the security stereotype and go with polos and khakis for our casual days and suits and ties for the more formal occasions. Darryl had chosen a navy blue polo and Joey a hunter green. I'd gone with my signature black and together we looked like a group of guys headed out to the golf course. I'd asked Joey to come along so I could see which person Ryanne felt most comfortable with especially since we were also guarding her son, Gage. Kids are funny and if he felt scared or intimidated, that would affect who got the assignment. They followed me to Ryanne's. Darryl was driving a deep blue Tahoe, and Joey was driving a charcoal Suburban. The gas bill was going to eat my budget, but it was something that needed to be done to keep the clients comfortable and safe at the same time. We pulled up at the house at 9:00 A.M. sharp, and I keyed in the code then watched as the gate swung open to allow us entry. We pulled up into the circular driveway and seeing the massive house again, I had to admit, it was a pretty impressive sight. I was climbing from the truck when I heard someone shouting. "Who in the hell did you hire? The damn secret service?"

I spun to find a guy I immediately recognized as 'THE' Rusty MacNeil stomping across the yard headed in our direction. He stopped when he realized we all towered over him by at least six inches. Rusty was a wiry, short man sporting a closely shaved haircut and icy blue eyes. He fixed those eyes on me, and I could see him puff out his chest as he finished his approach.

"So, you fellas are my wife's new security detail, huh?" He drawled. "I want you to know, this ain't how I do things. I had my own men doing this and she went behind my back to hire y'all. I'm not happy, not one bit." I could hear the anger rising in his voice as he continued. "Y'all boys are going to be in charge of the two most important people in my life and I'll be damned if you are driving off with her without meeting me first!"

There was a moment of silence then his face broke into a big grin. He slapped me on the shoulder and said, "I'm just messin' with ya. My wife runs me and this house and if you're good enough for her, then you're good enough for me!"

A moment later, Ryanne came out carrying Gage. "Rusty, why do you have to make an ass of yourself?" She admonished. "I'm so sorry, Ryder. He's been waiting on pins and needles for you to get here so he could mess with you. I begged him not to, but he's just a big kid."

Rusty put his arm around his wife and pulled her close. I noticed then that she was taller than him as well. The only person shorter than Rusty was Gage and by the looks of him, he was probably going to pass his dad by the time he was five. Rusty picked him up and gave him a big kiss.

I introduced Darryl and Joey to everyone and noticed immediately, that Gage was fine being around all of us. He garbled something that sounded like Barney and celery as he pointed at the guys, but I couldn't be sure.

"You be good for daddy today, okay?" Ryanne said giving him a kiss on his cheek. Turning to me she said, "I think we'd better get a move on. My appointment is at ten and I'm never late." She kissed

Rusty and watched as he carried Gage over his shoulder back into the house.

I seated her in the backseat, keeping her hidden from public view by the tinted windows. "So, where are we headed this morning?"

She glanced down at the paper in her hand. "I'm headed to the building at the corner of Russell and Greene. I have an appointment with Jolene Anderson in suite 14104."

I almost choked as she finished. "Jolene Anderson?"

She smiled. "Why yes, have you heard of her?"

I turned back to put the key in the ignition. "Well, yes, I have, and the ironic part is my office is located in the suite right next to hers."

Her mouth fell open. "What? That's too crazy! Well, I guess you don't need directions!"

We pulled up in front of the building and Joey and Darryl parked and met me at the car. As Ryanne emerged, a passerby stopped and stared and I knew she'd been recognized. She was a striking woman to begin with but also was a famous one at that. Within moments, cell phones were out and pictures being snapped. Joey and Darryl made a path to the door which Drake was holding open for us. Once safely inside, Ryanne turned to me and smiled. "Welcome to my world!"

I returned the smile. "We're ready!" The guys made sure the elevator was clear, and we rode in silence to the fourteenth floor. The doors opened, and we were greeted by a truly stunning Jolene. She was wearing a simple black dress paired with some sexy pumps. As she greeted Ryanne, I noticed how shapely her legs really were and those heels were driving me wild. I glanced up and found she'd caught me looking, and she gave me a little frown. All I could do was shrug and grin.

"Ms. Charles! I'm so happy to finally meet you," Jolene gushed as she held out her hand.

"Please, call me Ryanne! And I'm the one fangirling here. I've been a fan of yours for years and have many pieces from your collections. I almost fainted when my assistant told me you wanted to meet me!"

Jolene looked visibly shocked. "You're excited to meet me? Oh gosh! This is surreal! I'm a huge fan! I have your movie 'The Last Time' in my Blu-ray player and a box of tissues handy at all times. Oh, and please, call me Jolene." She led Ryanne into her office and after giving the guys the okay to just hang out at the office, I went into her office as well. Talk about convenience! This was a perfect job!

I sat in the outer office as they went into Jolene's conference room. Several others were already waiting for them, and I could see sketches scattered across the large wooden table. Olivia, who'd been serving coffee to the guests, came out, shut the door, and sat down at the desk.

"Can I get you anything?" She asked waving her hand toward the coffeemaker in the corner. "I have some fresh cookies as well!"

Shaking my head, I smiled. "You've got this job down pat already, don't you, Liv? It suits you."

She folded her hands in front of her on the desk. "I'm feeling it, so far," she said with a grin. "Plus the perk of free clothes is one I couldn't pass up." She studied me for a moment in silence then said, "So, while we're waiting, tell me what's been going on with you."

We hadn't spoken in a while so I filled her in briefly on my time in the Army and she, in turn, told me that she'd been at loose ends and that Jolene's return had been perfectly timed to get her focused on some sort of career path.

"I really didn't know what I was going to do. I went to college and came out with a piece of paper but no direction. At least now I have the security of a job and can explore what I want my degree in business to do for me," she said with a sigh.

I nodded in agreement. "I think that's why I joined the Army. I really needed something to get me on the right track. I found my calling and now I'm using my experience to hopefully set myself up for a career I'm going to love."

Olivia looked behind her to make sure the door was still closed. In a hushed tone, she said, "Between us, I think Jolene did the smartest thing by coming back home. After that piece of shit Marco did what he did, she needed to be around people who really care. And losing Giada has really shaken her to the core."

Who was Marco? I was intrigued. "Marco?"

Again she looked around keeping her voice low. "Marco Rinaldo. He was Giada's nephew and he and Jolene dated for two years until his greedy ass dumped her. He found out that she was going to have control over some of the company's hottest designs and that got his man-panties in a bunch. He walked out on her and hasn't been heard from since. Personally, if I ever see his sorry ass, I'll kick it right back out of town."

Interesting and good to know. She'd just had her heart stomped on and no doubt was skeptical of any man at this point.

"Ryder?" Olivia's voice got my attention. "She really needs someone stable…someone a lot like you. I know you've always liked her…have you ever thought of asking her out?"

I chuckled. "Well, as a matter of fact, I asked her out last night but honestly, I think she thinks I'm joking. I was as serious as a heart attack. It's been pretty obvious that I grew up having a crush on her but now I want to see where it could really go, if she would give me a chance."

She leaned back in her chair. "I can tell you, the Marco thing really messed with her head," she said seriously. "But I think if you can gain her trust, you may just get a happy ending out of it."

I was just about to say something else when the door to the conference room opened. There were smiles all around so I gathered everything had gone well in their meeting. Everyone was clustered around Jolene and Ryanne with words of praise, and they both had huge smiles on their faces.

"Jolene, these designs are fabulous!" An older woman was saying as she shuffled through some drawings in a portfolio. "We're so excited to be the first boutique in the area to carry them!"

"I'm so glad you like them, Ms. Abernathy!" Jolene said as she walked beside her. "With Ryanne Charles in the print ads and the point of purchase advertising, they're going to be eye-catching, that's for sure!"

Ryanne laughed. "Jolene, these clothes are amazing. I'm not the one making them great, you are!"

As they were saying their goodbyes, I checked my iPad and realized it was time to move on with Ryanne's next appointment. She was scheduled to do an interview with a local reporter about being the wife of a race driver and the trials of being apart so much. Ms. Rafe had forwarded her calendar to me, so I was able to coordinate things better.

Clearing my throat, I said, "Ms. Charles? We are ready to escort you to your next appointment."

Everyone stopped talking and looked at me. "Oh gosh," she said looking at her watch. "I'm so sorry." She turned to Jolene. "I will call you tomorrow about setting up fittings and we'll go from there. This is going to be a great experience, I can already tell."

As Ryanne joined me, she turned on the heel on her shoe and almost fell into me. I put my hand on the small of her back to steady her and saw Jolene watching us closely. We excused ourselves and as I was shutting the door, I heard Ms. Abernathy say, "Oh! If that's what security looks like nowadays, I'm getting a bodyguard right now!"

In the hallway, joined by my team, we headed back down to the lobby. "Ryder?" Ryanne asked with a giggle. "Do I really need three of you?"

"Well, actually, this first trip out was important to see what your danger levels are in the public. From what I can see, you're well received and don't seem to have the frenetic crazed fans that some celebrities do. I'm thinking that on a routine day, it'll just be one of us but when we have Gage with us, we'll have a team of two."

She nodded. "I like that plan. My husband either had too many men following me around or one really slack one who actually was more interested in getting an autograph from me to sell on eBay than protecting me. That was when I said to myself, enough is enough!"

I smiled. "Well, then so far, we seem to be in agreement about how things need to be handled. If you ever have any questions or concerns, please bring them to me, okay?"

With a nod, she walked through the entry doors and with our help, made it through the roughly sixty or so people who were jammed onto the sidewalk. I noticed there were now more professional cameras in the crowd meaning someone had tipped off the paps and that was not something I wanted to have to deal with. I made a note to keep her schedule as top-secret as possible to prevent any potentially dangerous situations, especially when she had Gage around.

As I drove away from the curb, I noticed a car following us and knew exactly what was going on. They wanted to know where she was going to be next, so they could camp out and possibly catch a great, or in some cases, horrible picture of her. Thankfully, the television station had a parking garage. As I pulled in, I made sure to tell the guard at the gate to make it hard for them to get in. He flashed a knowing smile, especially when he found out who was in the car, and we rolled in without our tail.

The interview took about an hour so while I was waiting, I caught up on some emails. I had several responses to my initial requests for clients as well as new ones who had *heard I was working for a "prominent celebrity"* and they wanted to schedule a meeting to discuss possibly handling them. I could already see I was going to need more employees so after responding to the emails with a *'I'll have someone contact you as soon as possible'*, I went through the resumes that I'd received and highlighted a few for further background checks, etc.

My phone chimed with a text from Ryanne.

I'm ready to be escorted! LOL

With a chuckle, I texted back.

10-4

I stood up and stretched then headed for the office where the interview had been held. My phone chimed again.

You hungry? I'm starved!

I checked the time and saw it was well after two. I knew she hadn't had time or the opportunity to grab a bite.

We'll grab some lunch on the way to the track.

Rusty was scheduled to do a radio interview for the network about an upcoming race, and he wanted Ryanne to join him. We had just over an hour before we needed to be there so I checked my phone for any quiet local restaurants in the immediate area. I found a family-owned pizza place right across the street.

Ryanne walked out the office as I texted our next stop to my team. I told her we could grab a quick bite over there before meeting up with Rusty.

She reached in her bag and pulled out a baseball cap and a huge pair of sunglasses. "I'm done for the day except for a radio interview so my hair be damned," she said laughing. "Let's go grab some eats!"

Ryanne was so down-to-earth and it constantly caught me off guard. She was just a normal person, and I guess I'd been guilty of lumping the celebs all in one big bunch of 'I'm better than you' snobs. We walked downstairs and after checking that the area was clear we made our way across the street to the restaurant.

As soon as we walked in, the hostess recognized Ryanne despite the disguise, but she kept her exuberance to a minimum when she saw me scanning the room for any potential problems. In a hushed voice, she said, "I can seat you right away, Ms. Charles." She led us to a table near the back of the softly lit room and handed us our menus. As she walked away, I watched her approach an older man who appeared to be the manager. After whispering in his ear, a big smile came over his face.

He made his way over to our table and in a low voice said, "I am Antony…owner and manager. We are honored to have you and your husband join us for lunch, Ms. Charles. Please accept your meal 'on the house'. It would be my honor."

Ryanne appeared puzzled for a moment, then I saw her bite her lip to keep from laughing. "Thank you but I would like to pay. In my profession, I get paid for my work and so should you." She flashed him a dazzling smile, and I actually saw him stumble a bit from his excitement.

"Well, please, let me get you a bottle of my finest wine, then. At least let me do that," he pleaded.

She considered it for a moment then smiled. "Sure, why not. I'm not driving!"

He rushed away and returned moments later with a bottle that he proudly displayed to her. "My papa brought thirty bottles of this with him from Italy and I've been saving each bottle for a very special occasion. This is one of those days!" He uncorked the wine and offered some to me but since I was on duty, as it were, I declined. Ryanne, however, pointed at her glass with another dazzling smile.

He carefully poured and she swirled, sniffed and sipped the wine like a pro. He smiled at her obvious experience and when she nodded her approval, he filled up her glass. He then snapped his fingers and a server magically appeared to take our orders. I quickly scanned the menu and found my favorite, Chicken Parmesan, so I ordered that and Ryanne nodded with approval. "I think I'll have the same."

Sipping her wine, we sat quietly listening to the background music and soon, the server was bringing our meals to the table. As we were about to eat, Ryanne picked up her glass and held it up for a toast. "To a great working relationship."

I picked up my water glass and clinked it to hers. We dug in to the delicious food and while we ate, she talked about how much she enjoyed the simpler life now that she'd stepped away from Los Angeles.

"I'll be honest, I jumped out of the frying pan into the fire with Rusty but I fell in love. He's got more fans than I could ever have. I've enjoyed having a normal life and when we had Gage it made things even better. Now, I'm feeling that itch to work again and I think working with Jolene will be just enough to take the edge off of my mundane life. I won't make it full-time again though, I want to have another baby someday and I can't see doing this with two to keep up with."

"Well, when the time is right, you'll make it work. My mother was a working mom and my brother and I turned out just fine." I felt my phone vibrate in my pocket, so I checked it and saw it was a text from Jolene. "I'm sorry. I hate people texting at dinner but I need to get this." She laughed and nodded as she took another bite of her dinner. I scanned the text.

I just wanted to let you know that I really do want to grab dinner sometime. My treat. I'd like to catch up and see what's new in your world. Are you free tonight? Let me know.

Smiling, I quickly texted back.

Sure, I'll call you later.

A few moments passed then a reply.

Sounds good!

I slipped the phone back in my pocket and saw Ryanne watching me closely. "So, is my schedule interfering with yours already?" She asked with eyebrows raised. "I don't want to be a clingy client."

"No, not at all. And besides, we're the ones who are supposed to be clingy. That's our job."

Ryanne and I finished our meals and when it was time to leave, the manager begged for a picture for his 'wall of celebrities'. Ryanne graciously obliged so they stood arm in arm in front of his father's picture and the server snapped a pic. We made our way out into the heat of the afternoon sun. Ryanne quickly pulled out her cap and sunglasses so we could make it back to the car without being mobbed. Once safely inside, we drove to the Charlotte Motor Speedway and after passing through security, we drove into the infield where Rusty's motor home was parked. It wasn't really a motor home though, more like a mansion on wheels. As we pulled up and parked, Ryanne looked over at my shocked face and laughed out loud. "Yes, it's pretentious and yes, it's too big but it's our home at the track and I don't think there's ever enough room to entertain a two year old. This is only one of several Rusty owns and he keeps them close to the bigger tracks and they drive them to whichever track he'll be at next."

I jumped out to open the door for Ryanne, and we heard a squeal. Rusty rounded the back of the motor home carrying a squirming Gage in his arms followed by a large man with an even larger belly. "Mama!" Gage giggled holding out his little arms toward his beaming mother.

Ryanne took him and gave him a big kiss. "Did you miss Mama today? She missed you!"

He nodded and said something that sounded like, "Cookie, all gone." She gasped and said, "No! We'll just have to get you another!"

She carried a waving Gage into the trailer and Rusty turned to me and grinned. "Damn, I love that woman. Did y'all have a good first day? Any problems?" I noticed that the large man had stationed himself at the side of Rusty.

"No, sir. We had no difficulties. We had a car follow us when we left the first appointment but I was able to stop them from following us to her television interview."

He reached up to slap me on the shoulder. "Good, good. I want her safe. She's the most precious thing in the world to me, next to my boy and I don't think I could stand anything happening to either one of them."

"Yes, sir. That's what we want too." The man was looking me up and down, and it suddenly hit me that this must me the 'security' that Rusty had protecting him. I returned his scrutiny and he finally looked away to presumably scan for threats.

Rusty smiled. "Well, we're all going home from here so my boys will keep an eye on us for the rest of the night." He glanced over at the guy who'd now puffed out his chest and attempted to suck in his ample waist.

With a smirk, I said, "Yes, I'm glad you have *heavy* security around you at all times." I turned, walked back to my car and headed back to the office.

Chapter 7

Jolene

Wow, I thought to myself as I shut the door behind Ryder and Ryanne. I closed my eyes and pictured him in his tight-fitting polo shirt, which emphasized his broad shoulders and muscular arms. He smelled so good too! Lucky Olivia had gotten to sit and chat with him while I carried out my business. I was so disappointed when Ryanne said during the meeting that she had another pressing appointment and they needed to leave. After they'd rushed out, I went back into the office, dropped down on the couch in Olivia's office and sighed. She stared at me, brows raised.

"What's up with you?" I finally asked after she said nothing for several minutes.

She rocked back in her chair and laughed. "Sis, you've got it bad."

"Excuse me?"

"Jolene Marie, you were literally drooling when you saw Ryder today." She dabbed the corners of her mouth with an imaginary napkin. "There's nothing to be ashamed of. He's looking mighty fine these days. I don't know why I never noticed him before."

As I glared at her silently, she laughed even harder. "I'm not interested, in case you're wondering. I just know there's some serious chemistry going on with you two since you both got back."

Shaking my head, I frowned. "No, he's not interested in me. Why would he be? He probably looks at me like…a good friend."

She frowned. "Honestly, I'm not so sure about that. I know for a fact he had a crush on you in the past. Why would you think that his feelings would change?"

I stood and threw my hands up. "Because I'm me…and he's him. Ah, hell, I don't know. Everything's so different now."

She walked over and patted me on the shoulder. "Listen, Ryder's fair game. He's not part of our family tree. Just because you've known someone all your life doesn't make them off limits."

I stood there silently. She was right. Why was I making this 'thing' between us bigger than it was? We were lifelong friends which in most relationship manuals was a good foundation for a future.

"So what do I do?" I whispered.

She reached over and picked up my cell phone. "Text him…"

I pushed the phone away. "I can't do that."

"Why not?" She asked as she started scrolling through my contacts. "If you won't, I will!"

"I don't know! I'm scrambling here!" I grabbed the phone from her. "I'll do it! Geez!" With trembling fingers, I typed in a text, making sure it didn't autocorrect me.

I typed, hit send, and then realized how stupid my message was. "Crap, crap! I should have reviewed my message. He's going to think I'm insane," I groaned.

"No, he won't!" Olivia said with a smug look on her face. "The ball's in his court now. Let's see how he handles it!"

My phone chimed with an incoming text and when I checked the message, I smiled.

"Yes?" Olivia asked anxiously.

"He said he'll call me later," I answered.

"Well, now he knows you're interested. 'Nothing ventured, nothing gained' as Dad always says."

"I guess so. We'll see."

Picking up her purse, she linked her arm in mine. "Well, don't sit around here waiting for him, how about taking your hungry sister out for lunch. I'm starving!"

All during lunch, I kept checking my phone to see if I missed any calls, which I hadn't. At the end of the day, I headed home, still hopeful he'd call. He didn't.

Later that night when I curled up on my balcony to enjoy the sounds of the city with a glass of wine in my hand, I decided to let fate handle my love life.

The next morning, my phone rang bright and early. I fumbled around for it and when I answered, all I could hear was Olivia chattering incoherently.

"Wait, slow down!" I said struggling to sit up and open my eyes.

"Okay," she said taking a breath. "I'm trying to prevent you from freaking out!"

"I just woke up," I said rubbing my eyes. "Why in the world would I be freaking out?"

Silence for a moment then she simply said, "Ryder's on that gossip website 'Exposed'."

Still confused about why this would freak me out, I climbed out of bed and turned on my iPad.

"I don't get this. First of all, why would a gossip site care about Ryder?" I said typing his name into Google. "He's not a celebrity or anything."

A moment later, the site popped on my screen and I saw a HUGE picture of Ryder and Ryanne Charles in a darkened restaurant clinking glasses. Another picture showed her touching his arm as they sat closely together. "Let me call you back," I said hanging up without waiting for a response.

The headline read "HAS RYANNE CHARLES DUMPED HUBBY FOR HOT BODYGUARD?" Stunned, I read the article.

Ryanne Charles has obviously gotten tired of hanging at the track. Sources tell us that Ms. Charles was spotted with her new hunky bodyguard at a Charlotte eatery. "They were sitting very close," one source revealed. "You could tell they were really into each other."

The owner of the restaurant who wished to remain anonymous, told us that he thought she was with her husband until one of the waitresses showed him a picture of Rusty MacNeil. "I mentioned her husband was with her and she didn't correct me so I assumed that's who he was."

Sources tell us that Ms. Charles was wearing a disguise, obviously to keep the public from finding out about her new boy toy but we at Exposed always find the truth. Stay tuned to see what comes next in their steamy new romance.

I looked at the grainy pictures and could see they were clearly enjoying themselves. Stomach clenching, I typed Ryanne Charles into the search bar and more grainy pictures popped up. One was taken outside our building when she'd arrived for her appointment. Another showed her climbing from Ryder's truck in an underground parking garage. He'd worked for her one day and already there were tons of pictures and stories about them being together.

My phone rang and was startled when I saw the number. It was Ryanne.

"Hello?"

"Jolene? It's Ryanne. I just had to call and let you know that some crazy stuff is being spread around in the tabloids but it is simply not true. I wanted to call you first thing to let you know because I don't want this affecting our working relationship. I can assure you that I would never cheat on my husband and don't want you to think any differently about me."

I got the feeling she was telling the truth but the images kept flashing through my mind. "Um, I just heard about it and haven't had a chance to read any of the stories," I lied. "I appreciate your calling me though."

She sounded really upset. "Well, I have to deal with an angry husband but these tabloids don't seem to care about that. Look, I need to go. Rusty is standing here so I'll just have to call you later and we'll talk."

"Okay." I said right before I heard our call disconnect. I dropped back onto the bed and replayed the conversation in my head. She really sounded upset…but…was that because she didn't do anything or because she got busted?

My phone rang again, and it was Olivia. "So, what do you think? Is it a thing or just a made-up thing? I thought you guys went out to dinner last night."

I sighed. "He never called. Liv, I don't know what to think. Ryanne just called me and assured me it was all a lie…but wouldn't she say that even if it wasn't a lie? She's not going to jeopardize her career by saying 'Oh yes, my hot bodyguard and I are an item and I don't care who knows'. She's going to do damage control and try to stop the rumors before they get out of hand."

Olivia was quiet. "Sis, I really don't know. You remember the actress who left her husband for the hot bodyguard? Nobody saw that coming."

"Yeah, I don't know what to think. Oh crap! Look at the time. We'll talk about it when I get to the office. Grab us some Starbucks and I'll see you there."

"Gotcha, Boss!"

An hour later, I had just turned on the computer and was checking the voicemail when the phone rang.

"Jolene Anderson," I answered.

"Ms. Anderson, this is Drake in the lobby. A man came in just a few minutes ago asking for you and when I picked up the phone to announce him, he slipped by me and got into the elevator. I wanted to let you know he may be there any minute now. I can't leave the lobby at the moment because several people are signing in."

"Uh, okay. I'm sure it's fine." Just as I hung up the phone, the door to my office slowly swung open.

My mouth fell open as I heard the words, "Ciao, bella mio," come out of the last person I expected to see.

Marco walked in holding out his arms. "Jolene. I'm so sorry. I hope I didn't startle you."

He wrapped me into his arms, but I didn't return the embrace. "Marco…what are you doing here?" I whispered.

"Where else would I be? Please forgive me. Io sono un bastardo. I wasn't thinking clearly. It was my grief. It took over my mind. Do you understand?" Releasing me from the hug, he held me at arm's length. "Tia Giada was very important to me and when she died…" He threw a hand over his heart. "It killed me inside."

My mind was whirling. "Marco. You did act like a bastard! You walked away from me without a word. I was hurting just as badly as you. I loved her like family too."

His dark brown eyes were pleading as he pulled me close again, and I felt myself soften against him. "Cara mia. Without you, my heart…it was broken, yes? I need you to make me whole again."

I felt him push the hair from my neck as his lips softly trailed my skin. One hand stroked my back as the other tangled in my hair. "Marco, wait," I said breathlessly. "I need a moment to think."

He shook his head as he looked into my eyes. "We've waited too long, Jolene. My passion for you is only growing. I want you in my life, in my bed. We make beautiful love together and I want that again."

"Excuse me? Do I need to call security?" Olivia was standing at the door holding our coffee, her eyes narrowed, and her lips in a frown.

I quickly backed away and in the process slammed the back of my legs against the desk. "Um, Olivia, this is Marco Rinaldo. Marco, this is my sister Olivia."

A smile spread across his face. "Ah, beautiful Olivia. Your sister told me of your beauty but mere words cannot describe how truly lovely you are."

Olivia's mouth dropped open. "Wha--?" She stammered.

Taking the coffee from her hand and setting it on the desk, he clutched her fingers and drew them to his lips. "A woman as beautiful as you would be most desired in my home country."

Olivia stood staring at him. "Wha--?"

Dropping Olivia's hand, he took mine turned it over, and kissed my palm. "I made the worst mistake of my life walking away from you. Without you, I am niente…nothing."

Olivia finally found her voice. "So you're the Marco that dumped her right after the will was read, huh? Good, I finally get to meet you in person…so I can kick your ass!"

Shaking his head, he held up his hand in defense. "Sadly, si. My mama always told me I have a terrible temper and sadly, I let it lead me away from my Jolene. I meant Jolene no harm. I can totally understand you wish to kick my ass."

I pulled my hand away, absently rubbing the spot where he'd kissed it. "Marco, I really don't know…I need some air." Grabbing my phone, I dashed out of the office, down the hall and into the elevator. The doors were closing when I saw a hand reach in to stop the door from shutting.

"Marco, I need—," I stopped speaking as I saw the doors part to reveal Ryder standing there.

"Marco?" He looked around seeing no one around, and he stepped into the elevator. "Are you saying that Marco is here?" I could see his jaw tighten.

I sighed. "Yes, he's here. Ryder, I can't talk about this right now." I busied myself with looking through my phone trying not to look at him. Too many questions were running through my head making it spin. "I'm sure you have more important things to do anyway."

"Jolene, nothing is more important than making sure you're okay. If this is about the tabloid—"

The elevator doors opened, and I made a dash for the front door. Over my shoulder I called back, "Ryder, what you do in your life is your business." Blinking back tears, I pushed through the doors right into a paparazzi storm.

"Ms. Anderson! Was that Ryder Brisson you were talking to? Are you aware of his relationship with your mutual client?" One reporter called out while another snapped pictures of me.

"There are reports that she's pregnant with his love child...can you confirm that?" Another shouted.

I pushed through the crowd and began running down the sidewalk. "Leave me alone!" I yelled while trying to figure out exactly where I was going to go. My condo was the other direction, and I really didn't want to go directly there and risk them following me. I rounded a corner and had enough of a lead that I was able to dart into a little bar without them seeing where I went. I found a stool at the back of the room and ordered a glass of wine to calm myself. My phone was ringing and chiming with texts, but I ignored it. I needed time to think and so far that wasn't happening.

Taking a sip from my wine, I felt my trembling begin to subside. Taking a deep breath, I sat there trying to sort out what had happened so far. Marco showing up was definitely a shock. Seeing him was bittersweet. The memory of how he walked out on me and how ruthless he'd become was still fresh in my mind. Then there was Ryder. Obviously, he wasn't the same person I knew when we were kids. He was all man and attractive as hell. What woman wouldn't want him? Closing my eyes, I pictured him that night at my condo, his blue eyes gazing intently into mine. I thought about what it would be like to kiss him. His lips were so inviting. Unconsciously, I licked my lips and heard a chuckle. I opened my eyes to see a familiar face.

"Sis, if you sit in a bar and lick your lips like that, you're going to have a riot on your hands!" Olivia said as she sat down on the stool next to me. She signaled for a glass of wine for herself and another for me. "By the way, thanks for leaving me with Casanova. He wouldn't stop talking about how much he loved you and how beautiful you were. I finally had to convince him to go back to his hotel with a promise I'd try to get you to call him. Fat chance of that happening but it worked."

I sighed. "I don't know what to feel right now. I'm kinda numb." The bartender put another glass of wine in front of me, and I took a big sip. "Marco…I just didn't expect to see him again."

She nodded. "And Ryder? He's stirred up some feelings, am I right?"

Cradling my head in my hands, I groaned. "He makes me feel…I don't know what. He's still Ryder and I can't quite process that."

She placed her hand on my shoulder. "Jolene…you have to get over this 'he's a kid' thing. He is a grown man who served our country and is now a businessman doing a dangerous profession. He's all man and no matter what the tabloids say, I think he's still got it bad for you."

"But I don't know what to do!" I whined.

She crossed her arms and leaned back. "If you're asking *me* what to do, then I say follow your heart. I know you and Marco were really close but I have a weird feeling about him. I can't put my finger on it but when I met him there was a definite red flag."

I rolled my eyes. "You're just saying that because you love Ryder. Marco was good to me for the two years we were together but then when Giada died…"

"So that makes it worse! What kind of man does that to someone he cares about? He tries to be all, 'Scusi, I no speak the English'. I call BS on that! He knew what he was doing when he climbed in his fancy car and left you standing there!"

Wearily, I shook my head. "It wasn't quite so dramatic."

Olivia stood abruptly. "Look, I heard you on the phone talking to Mom. You were wrecked. He was cruel and heartless and you were devastated. Now you're waffling about everything because he came back. I don't know what he's up to but I say it's no good!" She grabbed her purse, threw some money on the bar and stalked out.

A few minutes later, a man came to sit beside me. "You here alone?" He said leaning toward me.

Fighting the urge to smack him with my purse, I silently stood, tucked my purse under my arm, and walked out.

Luckily, I'd lost the mob, so I headed back to my condo. I unlocked my door, threw my keys on the entry table, kicked my shoes off, and I flopped onto the couch. I picked up the phone, checked the time and seeing it was early, called the one person I needed to talk to, Lucinda.

"Hello, babe," she said as she answered. "How's my favorite girl?"

"Not too good, I'm afraid," I said softly. "Marco's here."

"What the hell! What's he doing there?"

"I don't know. He just showed up today and started telling me how much he missed me and how wrong he'd been. I'm so confused and I needed to talk to you."

She paused. "Well, darling…how did it make you feel to see him? Angry? Sad? Did you want to snog him?"

"Lucinda!" I gasped. "Making out was the last thing on my mind. I couldn't even think straight when I saw him so I really can't tell you how I felt. Snogging was not on the list though."

She chuckled. "Well, then how did you feel?"

I sat there and thought about it. My first emotion had been anger. He'd felt like a stranger to me, and the tension between us had been palpable. Despite his declarations of love, his eyes were cold and distant. That was why I'd fled.

"When I first saw him, the first thing I thought of was how angry and upset I'd been the last time we'd been together. Lucinda, I can't let him hurt me again."

She cleared her throat then said, "Jolene. I love you like my own sister. I saw how he treated you and I was gutted. Any man that can walk away from someone they 'supposedly' had feelings for is a plonker in my book."

I sighed. "You're right. The sad part was I was on the verge of letting myself move on and he shows up again."

"Move on? Do tell!" She said excitedly.

I groaned. "Oh Lucinda, I don't even think there's anything to tell. You remember Ryder…"

"Ryder? My hot military mate? Of course, I do! He and I got along brilliantly!"

I hesitated for a moment then told her everything that had happened since we'd seen each other again. When I'd finished it was her turn to be silent.

"So," she said eventually. "You see him a little differently now, I take it?"

I hated to admit it but it was true. "Yes, I have feelings for him but the thing with the client has me all freaked out!"

"Look, darling. You've known him all of your life. Do you think he's the type of man to run around with a married woman?"

"No," I admitted, "I don't think he'd do that. I also don't see him jeopardizing his new security firm's reputation that way."

"Then you answered your own question, babe. He's worth giving the benefit of a doubt to," she said softly. "Give him a chance."

She was right. "You know, I love talking to you," I said with a smile. "You always make me feel better. Thank you for being my friend."

"You know I love you…now, I've got to get to bed. Trev is coming in the morning and we're going to Paris for the weekend. I've got a funny feeling that he's going to propose!"

I jumped up and squealed. "Oh my gosh! Lucinda! You have to call me as soon as he does! Please?!"

She laughed. "You'll be the first to know…after my mum and dad. Love you, babe!"

"Love you back! G'night!"

As I hung up, I heard a knock at the door. Puzzled, I walked to the peephole and looked out. I didn't see anyone, so I waited and listened for a moment before cracking the door open to see if anyone was in the hallway. On the floor, I found a bouquet of flowers. I looked to the left and right but didn't see anyone around, so I picked them up and took them inside. A card was nestled among the blooms so I plucked the card from the holder and opened the envelope.

You own my heart...you and you alone! With love, Marco

With a frown, I studied the card. Did he think this whole situation would go away with some flowers? A knock at the door startled me, and I dashed over to look outside again. He was standing there with a huge grin on his face holding a piece of paper that read, 'FORGIVE ME, CARA MIA'. I yanked the door open and glared at him.

"Marco, what are you doing? And how did you find out where I live?" I asked impatiently. "How did you get in my building?!"

"Jolene, I had to find you. I have ways of finding information. Money will buy anyone, or anything."

Shaking my head, I sighed, "Please just leave me alone. I can't deal with this right now."

He came toward me, holding his hands out. "Jolene, please don't break my heart in pieces."

My phone ringing mercifully gave me a temporary out. "I need to get that...please, just let yourself out." I grabbed the phone and answered it noting it was a blocked number as I did so. "Hello?"

"You know, I like watching you, Jolene," a deep man's voice said.

"Who is this?" I asked, puzzled.

"We'll meet soon enough," he growled. "You have what I want and I'm going to get it."

"Excuse me?" I said just as the call disconnected.

Marco was looking at me with concern. "Jolene, are you okay? You are so pale, Tesoro."

My hands were trembling as I set the phone down, and I quickly walked over to the windows and drew the curtains. "Um, I think it was a wrong number," I lied. "Please stop calling me your darling," I snapped.

He studied me carefully shaking his head. "It did not sound like that to me. You look upset."

I could feel tears brimming in my eyes, so I quickly blinked them back and took a deep breath. "I'm fine. I'm just really tired."

He nodded slowly, doubt still on his face. "Bene, I will take your word for it. Please, say you'll have dinner with me so we can talk. I beg for a chance."

Taking a deep breath, I started to say no but then I looked into his eyes and found myself saying yes.

"Tesoro, call me. That's all I ask. Grazie." He walked over to me, took my hand and kissed it softly. "I will count the minutes."

He turned and walked out leaving me even more confused than before. I was also puzzled and shaken by that phone call. I didn't recognize the voice, and it made me nervous. What had he meant by watching me? Shivering, I walked into my bedroom, pulling the drapes closed in there as well. The phone call really shook me but then the more I thought about it, the more I convinced myself that I'd overreacted. I'd already been agitated because of Marco, and I probably misheard what the caller had said. By the time I went to bed that night, I'd dismissed the call altogether as just my crazy nerves.

Chapter 8

Ryder

Taking a sip of coffee while I waited for Ryanne to come out of the house, I thought about Jolene and Marco. It had definitely rocked me to hear he was in town and had paid a visit to Jolene. It had definitely been a crazy week. First of all, the tabloids jumping to conclusions had not made my life easy by any means. I had to assure Rusty that everything that had happened between Ryanne and I was strictly professional. When he looked at the photos again, he saw my team in the background (obviously not pointed out by the scum reporting it) and in the restaurant it was obvious that we were having lunch not canoodling in a corner. It did make me more aware of my positioning when Ryanne and I were together to keep these kinds of reports from happening again.

Secondly, I now had an ex of Jolene's lurking around. Olivia assured me that it was over between them but the look on Jolene's face in the elevator had been one of emotional distress. She was trembling and I saw tears in her eyes, but she'd obviously not wanted me to see. I was lucky in one sense. Ryanne was working with Jolene now on the new line and was going to be at her office every day, which meant I was as well.

My thoughts were interrupted by Ryanne opening the door to climb in. "I'm sorry I'm late. Gage was in a bad mood this morning and didn't want to stay with Rusty but it's just not a take your two year old to work day. He's not racing this week so he's going to take him out on the boat and keep him occupied for the day."

We drove in silence for a while then I heard Ryanne clear her throat. "Ryder, please don't treat me any differently because of what's happened. This is the kind of crap I ran away from when I left Hollywood and really didn't think it would follow me here but they'll get tired of me and eventually find some other poor victim to prey on."

Looking into the rearview mirror, our eyes met. I could see she was hurt by everything that happened and I felt so sorry for her having to live in a fishbowl. "It's okay, Ryanne. I just don't want any of that to affect your family. I'm on my own and can handle that but when they insinuate that a married woman with a child is having an affair, it really pisses me off, pardon my language."

She laughed, leaned forward and put her hand on my shoulder. "It pisses me off too! I think the hardest thing for me is having to try to explain things to Rusty. Even though he's in the public eye, most of the time, he's around other guys in the garage and at the track."

"Well, just to let you know, from now on, I'll be more aware of our proximity. I don't want anyone ruining your life just because I happened to be walking a little too close to you."

Our conversation halted as we pulled up in front of the building. I motioned for Ryanne to wait as I climbed out and scanned the area for any trouble. The paparazzi were noticeably absent, which gave me cause to be concerned. My instinct was telling me that they were probably hiding in the bushes or behind a parked car waiting to catch us off guard. My team arrived and formed their corridor, and I opened the door. As soon as I did, I heard a click and saw a large lens poking from a car parked nearby. I blocked their shot with my body, and Joey took Ryanne by the arm and led her into the building.

I heard footsteps approaching and turned to see a few reporters milling around behind me. "So, do you want to make a statement?" One of the reporters yelled at me.

"Is she as good in bed as I think she is?" Said another. I clenched my fists and glared at them.

Without a word, I turned and went into the building. Ryanne and Joey had already gone up and Drake was leaning against the counter shaking his head. "I've never seen anything like this," he said as he signed me in. "Those guys are nuts! I've had people calling me all morning asking me what time she comes in. I told them to go to Hell."

I slapped Drake on the shoulder. "Thanks, man. The sad part is, this is common for her. Can you imagine?"

He shook his head. "No, I really can't. I'm nobody and they've been following me out the building when I get off work asking me personal questions about Ms. Anderson too."

My body tensed instinctively. "What kind of questions?"

He glanced around to make sure no one was nearby. "Well, a guy has been hanging around, some Italian guy, and the word is they were an item. The paps think they're rekindling. They ask me if he comes here a lot and if they leave together. I tell them I don't know anything and leave it at that."

Taking a deep breath to calm myself, I said as evenly as I could, "And are they?"

Drake considered it for a moment then shook his head no. "In my opinion, I'd say he's uninvited. Now, I may be wrong but that's just my gut feeling."

My phone chimed with a text, and I quickly checked to see who it was. Joey was checking in.

Ms. Charles is safely in Ms. Anderson's office. Darryl and I are going to do some paperwork and she said she'd let us know when she's ready to leave.

I texted that I'd be up in a few minutes. "Drake, if you hear or see anything you think is out of the ordinary, let me know. These reporters are tenacious and will stop at nothing to get a story or a picture."

He smiled. "You can count on me!"

I rode the elevator to the office and saw Olivia going into Jolene's door. "Hey Ryder!" She said waving. I waved back and went into my office. Joey and Darryl were discussing the logistics of an upcoming fashion show that Maxine and Jolene had planned for later this month. The press had begun covering the show extensively, especially since it would be Ryanne's return to modeling along with the debut of Jolene's own line which was highly anticipated.

"So, I think we need to have someone backstage with the models," Darryl said with a wink. "I'll bite the bullet and take the assignment.

Joey rolled his eyes. "Sure, you want to be with the models. I'm sure I'm going to be watching the kid." He looked over at me with raised eyebrows. "That's my assignment, isn't it, Boss?"

I laughed. "Joey, you *are* really good with Gage." I looked at the schedule they had been going over. "Hm, Rusty's going to be out of town this week so I'm sure we'll have Ryanne and Gage. I think that Gage is best with you, Joey. He likes you. I am, however, going to be the one in the back with the models. Darryl, you'll be in the audience with the fans in case one goes wacky on us."

Darryl frowned with disappointment until I reminded him that according to the paperwork, several celebrities would be in attendance, and his whole attitude changed. Running his finger down the list, he whistled. "Okay, man…I'm on board for the audience."

We talked over a few more details and then I left them mapping out the schedule for the rest of the week. Closing my office door, I sat down and pulled a file up on my computer. Clicking it open, I studied the face staring back at me. I'd been doing some checking on him ever since Olivia told me about him. Marco Rinaldo was Italian, born and raised in Genoa, and the only child of Giuseppe and Arabella Rinaldo. Giada, Guiseppe's younger sister had never married but had been involved with some of the most famous bachelors in the world. I discovered tragedy seemed to follow their family. Their oldest brother, Marcelo had been killed in a skiing accident when he was just a teenager. Marco is thirty, has never been married and apparently is very wealthy due to his aunt's inheritance. I found photos of him and Jolene when they were in London, mostly taken at nightclubs and fashion shows. I found a link to the story of their breakup and read with interest.

Romance on the Rocks!

It seems talented young designer, Jolene Anderson, and her hot Italian lover, Marco Rinaldo, have gone their separate ways. Sources tell us that following the untimely death of his aunt, Giada Rinaldo, Marco backed away from their relationship as soon as he found out the designs done by the talented Ms. Anderson were not part of his inheritance. A close friend told us that she was devastated and that's when she decided to run back home to her native North Carolina. Marco flew back to Italy and within days was seen at a local nightclub throwing money around to beautiful women. The champagne was flowing and it was obvious to this reporter that he wasn't dwelling on the breakup. We'll keep you up to date on the latest news!

The story had the now familiar grainy photo showing Jolene talking to Marco outside a café and the next photo showed him sitting in his car as she stood nearby crying.

A knock at the door startled me, and I quickly minimized the file and yelled, "Come in."

Joey poked his head in the door. "Ryder, Ms. Charles is ready to leave."

"Okay, I'll be right there." I closed the file completely and shut off my computer. Grabbing my keys, I made my way to the office next door. Ryanne was saying her goodbyes and my eyes locked onto Jolene, who looked absolutely gorgeous. She had her hair piled up in a bun, and she was wearing a pair of skinny jeans with a t-shirt.

"Ryanne," she was saying as I walked up. "Don't forget that the final fitting is in two weeks and the actual show starts at four on the following Tuesday. We should plan to be at Maxine's by noon that day."

She nodded and gave her a hug. I was just about to escort Ryanne downstairs when Jolene said, "Ryder, can I talk to you for a minute?"

"Sure," I said motioning to Darryl and Joey to take over. "I'll be down in a minute."

Ryanne smiled and nodded as they walked to the elevator. Jolene stepped out of her office and shut the door leaving us alone in the hallway. Her sweet fragrance surrounded me, and I found myself breathing deeply to take it in. "So, I want to apologize for being so abrupt yesterday. I…I wasn't myself."

"Okay…" I said. "What happened?"

She leaned against the wall, and I felt the urge to step closer but had to resist. It was driving me crazy not to be able to touch her. "Well, first of all, what happened the other night? You said you were going to call and I never heard from you."

I told her the truth. "I'm so sorry about that. I came back to the office to catch up on some paperwork and by the time I looked at my watch, it was midnight. I couldn't call you then so I decided to wait until the next morning to explain. I woke up to my phone blowing up from all the texts and phone calls about the tabloid crap. I decided the best thing was to come to you in person and explain but when I went to talk to you, you were escaping from Marco."

She considered it for a moment then nodded. "I have to admit I was disappointed."

"I'm so sorry, Jolene. Believe me I wanted to see you. I also have to ask…what happened with Marco?"

She took a deep breath then said, "I guess by now, you must have heard I dated him while I was in London. Well, we had a bad breakup and I hadn't seen him since Giada's will was read. He showed up out of the blue and to be honest, it really freaked me out."

I studied her face. "So, do you still have feelings for him? Is that why it freaked you out?"

She blushed and looked away. "No, I…I don't. I honestly don't know what to feel. I thought I loved him but he turned into someone completely different and it was all over money. I'm having a hard time believing he's suddenly changed."

"He says he's changed? How?" I asked.

Still looking away, she said, "He says he still loves me and that he made a mistake. He wants me back and I just feel that he's…I don't know…different."

Taking her chin in my hand, I turned her to face me. "Jolene, your gut is your best guide in life. It has helped me make a lot of difficult decisions in my life and it can help you do the same. I can't tell you if you should trust this guy. I don't know him. What I do know is you're a smart, strong woman and you will make the right choice." I caressed her cheek with my thumb. "Personally, I'm hoping that one day, you'll give me a chance."

A strange look crossed her face. "But—," she stopped speaking and just looked up at me, tears welling in her eyes.

"But what?" I asked stepping a bit closer as I tilted her chin up, so I could look into her sapphire blue eyes rimmed with her long, full lashes.

"Ryder, I'm scared," she whispered.

Our bodies were now just inches apart. Looking into her eyes, I asked softly, "Scared of what?"

She blinked quickly and licked her lips. "I'm scared of someone hurting me again."

I frowned. "Do you honestly think I would hurt you?"

She placed her hand on mine and pulled it away from her face. She stepped out of my reach and backed to the door of her office. "You'd better go." Her voice trembling, she said, "Ryanne is waiting." She turned the knob, walked through the door and closed it firmly behind her.

In frustration, I pounded my fist on the wall. "Damn it. What did he do to her?"

Taking one last look back at her door, I boarded the elevator and joined up with my crew and my client.

Later that night, after making sure Ryanne was safely home with Rusty, I went back to the office to do some last minute paperwork. As I was getting off the elevator, I noticed Jolene's door was ajar. The main lights were off, but the desk lamp on Olivia's desk was on. I pushed the door open and found the office had been vandalized. The computer screen had been smashed. The chairs flipped upside down, and the file cabinets rifled through. Olivia's desk had been cleared obviously with a sweep of a hand leaving all of her papers strewn on the floor. Jolene's design cabinet had been pried open, and some of her drawings ripped in half. Stunned, I grabbed my phone and dialed her number.

She sounded half asleep when she answered. "Um, hello?" She murmured.

"Jolene, it's Ryder. I don't want to alarm you but something's happened at your office. You've been broken into and someone has destroyed some of your important papers and drawings."

"Oh! I'll be right there!" She gasped.

"No. You stay put. I'm going to call your alarm company and figure out why it didn't go off and then I'll get the locksmith to come fix your lock. You don't need to be out wandering around late at night."

"Ryder!" She protested. "I think I should come in!"

"No, if you want, I'll come by after it's all taken care of and make sure you're okay."

She sighed. "Okay. I won't be able to sleep anyway so just come over when you can."

I hung up the phone and called the alarm company. They had no explanation for the alarm not being triggered and assured me they'd be out the next day to check it. I called a 24 hour locksmith who came out in less than thirty minutes to fix the door. While they were doing that, I looked around the office to see what, if anything, was missing.

A piece of paper caught my eye. It was laying by the door to Jolene's office. I picked it up and opened it to see a computer printed note.

I'm watching you, Jolene. Now that I've been in your office, I want more.

I folded the note carefully and set it on the desk to give to the police as soon as they arrived. This seemed to be the work of a stalker from the sound of things. I checked my watch, and it was just after two when I pulled the door to her office shut and checked to make sure it was locked.

I arrived at Jolene's about ten minutes later, and she buzzed me in as soon as I rang the intercom. I dashed up the steps, and she met me at the door. "Is everything okay?" She asked as she let me into her condo. "I wanted to come down there and see it for myself."

I could see she was trembling so I pulled her into a hug. "They trashed your office and broke a few things that can be fixed. The good thing is that no one got hurt."

"But why?" She asked looking up into my eyes, tears dampening her lashes.

I'd debated on the way over whether or not to tell her about the note but common sense told me to so she's aware someone was targeting her.

"Well, we found something that may shed some light on the why, but not the who." I showed her a picture of the note the police had kept for evidence. She read it to herself.

"Ryder, this scares me," she said, her eyes wide.

I pulled her back into a hug. "I know."

She pulled back. "No, Ryder…this really scares me." She began pacing in front of me. "I got a weird call from someone who said he liked watching me and that I had what he wanted. I thought it was just someone playing around or that I misheard it but now I think this is the same person."

"Did their number show up on your phone?" I asked as I walked over to pick up her cell.

"No, they had the number blocked. Marco was here when they called but I didn't say anything to him about it."

I spun when I heard Marco's name. "Oh really? And what was he doing here?"

She closed her eyes and her shoulders slumped. "Ryder, he came by to try to talk to me but I told him to leave. He's just confusing me. I don't know what to do with him."

Thoughts of what I could do to him popped in my head and none of them were pleasant or painless. "Jolene, I wish you would have told me about the phone call."

She nodded. "I know. I'm pretty stupid sometimes." She gave me a soft smile. "Thank you for everything tonight. I'm glad you were there."

Taking that as a cue, I took her by the arm and led her to the couch. "Listen, we need to talk." She sat down, and I sat on the ottoman in front of her. Taking her hands in mine, I said, "Jolene, this whole situation worries me. You really need to think about protection. If someone has targeted you, it may not be just vandalism next time. He obviously has your phone number and from the note, it sounds as if he knows where you live. I don't like it."

She bit her lip nervously and despite the serious situation, I couldn't help but let my eyes linger there. "Well, the only person I would ever trust to do that for me is you and you're already tied up with a client."

"Jolene," I said circling my thumb across the back of her hand. "I wouldn't trust anyone else either. I've just hired two new employees so I can let Darryl and Joey take care of Ryanne and Gage. I want to be the one to protect you."

She nodded as she blinked back tears. "Thank you," she said softly.

I stood, pulled her to her feet and held her close. "It'll be okay," I said, stroking her back. "I won't let anyone hurt you."

She pulled away but stayed in my arms. "Ryder, I—," She didn't say anything else, just stood on her toes and gently kissed my lips. It was electric. Instantly, her face flushed and she looked away as if embarrassed. Taking her chin in my hand, I turned her back to face me. I leaned in and saw the surprise in her eyes as my lips pressed to hers. Her eyes fluttered shut, and she moaned softly as she pressed against me. I didn't want it to end. Finally, she pulled away and the moment was gone. "I'm so sorry. I don't know what came over me," she said averting her gaze.

"Don't be sorry, Jolene. I've wanted to do that for a long time." I brushed the hair back from her face.

Taking a deep breath, she looked at the clock. "Gosh, it's really late. You'd better get home so you can get some sleep. I've got a busy day ahead of me anyway. What's the plan?"

It was very obvious she felt totally awkward about what had just happened but I also knew she'd felt something. I played it cool. "Well, I'll call Ryanne in the morning and get her set up with the guys and I'll be here to pick you up at…what time do you go in?"

She laughed nervously. "Really…you don't have to pick me up. It's not that serious…is it?"

"Yes," I insisted. "I have a feeling these messages are just the beginning and I don't want this guy to get anywhere near you."

She finally nodded. "Okay, I usually leave for the office at 8:30. I'll be ready then."

"Got it. Jolene, I know this is for the best. At least until we figure out who's sending these messages." I turned and went toward the door but stopped and looked back. "If you need me, I'm just a phone call away. Now lock your door."

She walked to the door and as she shut the door behind me, she said softly, "Goodnight, Ryder."

Chapter 9

Jolene

After locking the door and the deadbolt, I leaned against the door. Ryder had shaken me with the news of the break in but when he'd taken me in his arms, I'd felt so safe. The kiss had been totally spontaneous on my part but when he kissed me back, I hadn't expected the rush of feelings that came along with it. I wanted him.

Dragging myself to the couch, exhausted by everything that had happened, I curled up in a ball and soon fell into a fitful sleep.

My phone woke me, and I looked at the time and panicked. It was almost eight, and I wasn't even remotely ready for work. I grabbed it and saw it was Marco calling. I declined the call then grabbed a quick shower opting to go for casual Friday in every sense of the word. I pulled on some comfy capris and a bright pink blouse covered in white polka-dots. It was one of my favorites. Secretly, I wanted to look good for Ryder. I quickly braided my hair leaving it draped over my shoulder and applied some light makeup.

At 8:30 sharp, my intercom rang. I was just about to push the button to let Ryder in when I realized that I was just assuming it was him. "Yes?" I asked.

"Jolene, it's Ryder," he said firmly.

I buzzed him in and within a few moments, he was knocking at my door. I checked the peephole to be sure and let him in.

His eyes were scanning the room, but I also saw him give me the once over which made me feel good that I'd taken the extra time on my appearance. "Any problems?" He asked.

"No, I fell asleep on the couch after you left and stayed there until my phone rang this morning." I picked up my phone and saw Marco had left a voicemail.

Ryder saw it too and frowned but didn't say anything. "Well, we'd better get going. Lock up and we'll go down to the car."

As we came downstairs, one of my neighbors who'd always been friendly waved at me, and I waved back. Then I realized he was waving to get me to come over to talk to him. Ryder tensed, but I shook my head indicating he was okay. "Mr. Beck," I said smiling. "How are you this morning?"

He smiled and looked with interest at Ryder who was dressed in his customary black polo and khakis. "Well, Jolene, I wanted to give you this package. It was delivered yesterday but you were still at work and I didn't trust them leaving it by your door so I signed for it. I was planning to bring it up to you but ended up taking a nap with my lazy cat, but…here you are! You saved me a trip up the stairs for which I'm most grateful."

He handed me a package and the first thing I noticed was there was no return address. Ryder also noticed and quickly took the package from my hands. He looked it over carefully then said, "Stay here. I'll be right back."

He left Mr. Beck and me standing there. I felt a little awkward, so I asked about his wife, and he caught me up on her latest ailments. A few minutes later, Ryder came back in without the package and with a forced smile, pulled me away with the excuse that we were running late. He opened the back door for me. "Why do I have to sit in the back? I asked with confusion.

"All of my clients ride in the back," he explained holding out his hand to help me in.

"But I'm your friend! I don't want to sit in the back like a dork."

He sighed. "Jolene, the windows are tinted in the back. It gives you some protection from view. Please, let me keep you safe."

After he put it like that, I climbed in the SUV and noticed the box was open in the back of the truck. I started to look, but Ryder shook his head. "No, don't touch it. We'll talk about it when we get to your office."

Perplexed, I sat back and tried not to let my anxiety get the best of me. Ryder slipped on a pair of dark sunglasses, so I couldn't see his eyes. His face showed no emotion, and it was making me even more nervous.

When we arrived at our building, he parked at the front door and motioned for me to stay put. After he'd scanned the area, he opened the back door, grabbed the box and then opened my door. I hopped out and we quickly made our way into the building. Drake was working and seemed surprised to see me with Ryder. He quickly waved us in, and we went up to my office. Once safely inside, Ryder went straight to my office as I followed closely behind. He placed the box on the desk and turned toward me, blocking my view of the box.

"Ryder, you're scaring me," I said anxiously. "What's in the box?"

He hesitated then stepped aside to let me see. Inside the box was a note written in big block letters. It read 'I MUST HAVE YOU' on one line pasted above a picture of me taken from a magazine article. Underneath my picture was another message 'SOON'.

My hands grew clammy, and I felt the room spin. Ryder put his arm around me to steady me. Using a pen, he carefully lifted the note to reveal a stack of pictures of me. Some were cut from newspapers or magazines and some were obviously taken recently outside my office. One picture made me feel nauseous as soon as I saw it. "Ryder, this was from two days ago." It was taken from across the street with a high powered camera but it was definitely me, and I was wearing my pajamas.

He frowned. "This confirms he's definitely watching you." He dropped the note back into the box. "I'm going to give this to the police. They'll want to see this after the break-in. Our mystery man has been busy." He put his arms around me. "Jolene, this means you can't be left alone. I'm going to have to be with you 24/7 until we figure out who this is."

We were interrupted by raised voices coming from the outer office. "Look! You can't go in there!" Olivia was shouting.

The door swung open. "I must see her!" It was Marco, and his eyes narrowed as he saw me wrapped in Ryder's arms. Without thinking, I quickly stepped back and saw a strange look on Ryder's face as I did so. "Jolene, I just heard someone broke into your office. Amore, thank God you weren't hurt!" He rushed over to take me into his arms. "I don't know what I would do if anything happened to you!" He brushed his lips against my cheek. "Ti amo!"

I pulled myself from his embrace. "You love me? Marco, seriously?" Ryder was watching us carefully. "You seem to think I can just forget everything that's happened."

Marco glared at Ryder. "Could we be alone?" He asked.

Ryder considered it for a moment then shrugged and said, "Nope."

Marco scowled at Ryder then turned to me. "Jolene...I admit I was foolish but can you punish me for life? I want us to be together...like we were. We can fly to Italy and you'll be safe there. I want to marry you! Tia Giada would want that. Together we can rebuild the House of Rinaldo and the only way I want to do it is with you by my side." He cupped my cheek with his hand and said softly,

"Don't you remember our nights together when we made love? You said you loved me then."

My face flushed. It was obvious he was saying these things in front of Ryder to stake some sort of claim on me, but it was only making me embarrassed and mad. "Marco, stop it! I'm done with the past. I've moved on."

He regarded Ryder with a frown. "With him? Jolene, you can't want someone like him," he seethed. "He doesn't know you like I do. Per favore, please? Let me take you to dinner. Let me explain my heart." He grasped my hand and placed it against his chest. "My heart aches for you. If you don't want me after I explain, I promise I will leave."

Closing my eyes, I sighed. Even though I knew it was a mistake, I had to quit running from the situation and end it with Marco once and for all. "Okay. I'll give you the chance to explain but remember, I *will* hold you to your promise." Ryder's jaw clenched but he said nothing.

"Good. I'll pick you up at seven—," He was interrupted by Ryder clearing his throat.

With his eyes locked on me, Ryder said, "Excuse me but I'm Ms. Anderson's full-time security. I will be escorting her wherever she goes so *we* will pick *you* up at seven. Where are you staying?"

Marco stepped toward Ryder. "You are coming with us?" He hissed as he balled up his fist and began shaking it at Ryder. "I want my woman to myself!"

Ryder smiled. "Sorry, dude. First of all, she's under my protection and that's not negotiable. Second, I think she just made it clear that she's *not* your woman."

Marco's chest heaved as he clenched his fists and muttered under his breath, "Bastardo!"

Ryder held his hand behind his ear. "Mi scusi?" With a grin he shrugged his shoulders. "I speak a few languages, just so you know."

Marco took a deep breath to calm himself then walked toward me and kissed both of my cheeks. "I'll make reservations at Antonio's. I yearn for my native food. I'm staying at the Ritz-Carlton. Until tonight, ciao bella."

Smiling Ryder said, "Make sure the reservations are for a party of three."

With a final glare, Marco stalked out slamming the door behind him. There was an awkward silence until Ryder said with a chuckle, "You know, I get the feeling from Marco that I'm not welcome."

Shaking my head, I burst out laughing. "I can't imagine why." The direct line to my office rang. "Hello?"

"I'm watching you," a raspy voice whispered. My eyes snapped to Ryder, and it was as if he could read my mind. He mouthed '*is that the creep?*' to me and when I nodded, he motioned to keep him on the phone, and he went into Olivia's office to pick up the other extension.

"Who is this?" I demanded. "This isn't funny. You're watching me now?"

"Yes, and I'm not happy," he growled. "I want you to get rid of those men. I'm the only one you need and I will have you…or no one will! You've been warned!"

Trembling, I sputtered, "I'm sorry but—" The phone went dead.

Ryder came back into the office. "Did he hang up already? I was going to try to get the phone company to trace the call."

"He knew about you and Marco," I said putting the receiver down. "He said to get rid of those men."."

Ryder abruptly turned and went back out to the front office. "Olivia, I need you to cancel all of Jolene's appointments for today. You're both going home early and I'm taking her out of here." He came back into the office and before I could protest, he grabbed my things and taking me by the arm, led me out. "Jolene, if he's here you don't need to be." He called his other employees and alerted them that he was leaving. He instructed someone named Mason to bring the SUV to the door.

After Olivia had made the necessary calls, we rode down with her in the elevator, with Ryder's hand still clutching me tightly. When the doors opened, he moved in front of us and looked out, making sure there was no danger before walking out. He pulled me along past Drake, who was standing slack-jawed as we ran through the lobby. When we reached the doors, he made sure the car was waiting, then we dashed from the doors and we climbed into the back. Joey stuck his head in. "Ryder, what do you need me to do?"

"Make sure Olivia gets safely to her car, would you?"

"You got it!" He said before turning to her. "So, where are you parked?"

As they walked off, a tall, muscular man with long dark hair, wearing the same clothing as Ryder climbed in the driver's seat. Ryder leaned forward to speak to him and with a sharp nod, he pulled away from the curb. Both of them were constantly checking behind us until we left town. "Where exactly are we going?" I asked anxiously.

Ryder glanced at me and said very seriously, "My place."

I was confused. "Why are we going there? My condo is closer," I argued.

Shaking his head, he said with surprise, "You're not serious...your condo? The guy already knows where you live. Your deadbolt isn't going to stop someone determined to get in. It would be safer for us to go to my house until we can completely secure your place."

"You have a house?" I was astonished.

"Yeah, I bought it a year ago. My dad did all the negotiating for me and I just made the payments. Nobody knows where it is except those closest to me." He leaned forward to speak to the driver. "Mason, let us out up ahead. I want you to head back to town and get started on securing Jolene's place."

Mason nodded and pulled over to allow us to get out. Ryder turned to me. "Jolene, give him your keys." I dug around in my purse and pulled out my keys then lay them in Mason's open palm. Ryder quickly gave Mason the address to my condo, and we climbed out by a gated driveway. "Come," Ryder said taking my hand.

After pressing the security code, the gates opened and we walked through. The driveway was long and led to a beautiful two story house set among a dense patch of trees. Ryder was still holding my hand and he turned to me. "Do you like it?" He asked, with a tentative smile.

It was breathtaking. My eyes wide, I nodded slowly. "Ryder, it's gorgeous!"

He led me onto the porch, which wrapped around the entire house. Several white rocking chairs lined the porch interspersed with huge ferns. Wind chimes gently swayed in the wind making soft music. Ryder released my hand then pulled his keys from his pocket and unlocked the door. Motioning for me to wait, he entered and disarmed his alarm. He came back to the door and taking both my hands, backed into the house pulling me with him.

My eyes swept over the open foyer with the grand staircase leading to the second floor. Its southern charm was evident in every detail, and I fell in love with it right away. Ryder led me to the den, which boasted cozy leather couches with matching ottomans and a huge flat screen television mounted over a massive stone fireplace. "Make yourself at home. I've got to make some calls," he said giving me a gentle hug. "My place is your place."

He walked into a room off the den that appeared to be an office and gently shut the door behind him. The couches looked so inviting, and I was just about to sit down when something on the bookshelf caught my eye. As I got closer, I could see it was a picture of me taken the summer our families went to Carolina Beach together. It was right before I left for London, and I remembered Ryder had gotten a new camera for his birthday and insisted he try it out on me. Wearing a big floppy hat, I'd posed with bucket and spade in my hand. It surprised me that he had this picture framed and sitting on his bookshelf among all of his important manuals. Smiling, I turned as he came back into the room. Right away, he saw what I'd been looking at.

"That's my favorite picture," he said walking over to pick it up. "I took this with me overseas. All the guys wanted to know who you were and to be honest, most times, I told them you were my girl." He turned away but kept talking. "There were nights when I would lay awake in my bunk and wish I could talk to you. You and I had always been so close but as we got older, I felt you pushing me away. I guess I was just a dorky kid in your eyes…"

I started to speak, but he continued. "I came to England to see you but you were gone. Lucinda told me how famous you were becoming and I realized our worlds were so different that any chance I had at being more than a friend was nonexistent. I headed back to the base and put your picture away, finally convincing myself that you were just a silly crush. But you never left my mind completely. I always wondered where you were and what you were doing and thankfully, it was always the topic of discussion when I was with your family. I found out you'd become a famous designer, and had pretty much decided to stay in London." He turned to me, and our eyes locked. "Then my mom told me you'd moved back here. All the feelings I'd been denying came rushing back. You know how I've always felt about you, Jolene. And I also know you don't feel the same way, and I can accept that. I just want you to be happy and safe and I'll do anything in my power to make that happen."

I stood there totally speechless. My heart was screaming 'TELL HIM YOU FEEL SOMETHING FOR HIM!' but my head was saying 'Don't play with his heart. Don't ruin a great friendship.' I'd already crossed a line by kissing him, and it had only made things more confusing. I opened my mouth to try to explain how I was feeling but was interrupted by his phone ringing.

I could tell it was one of his guys and they were talking about Ryanne and her security.

When he hung up, he said, "So, are you still planning to go to dinner with what's-his-name?"

"Look, you may not like him but I did have a relationship with him and I feel I owe it to him to hear him out." I turned on my heel and headed to the door. Pointing out my jeans and t-shirt, I said, "Unless you have something appropriate for me to wear tonight, I suggest you take me home so I can get ready." I could see the hurt in his eyes but I needed to back off.

"You're not going anywhere right now. Mason's at your place getting some new security installed and until he calls, you're stuck with me."

I huffed and spun around. "Well, crap!"

He narrowed his eyes. "What's going on? Why are you so pissed?" He asked taking a step toward me.

Closing my eyes, I said, "Is there something going on with you and Ryanne?"

He stared at me with his brows raised. "Where in the hell did that come from?"

I turned to look out the window. "Ryder, you're an attractive guy. Who wouldn't be interested in you? I'm sure Ryanne sees what everyone else does."

He exhaled in a deep sigh. "You believe those sleazy tabloids," he said softly.

Still facing the window, I said, "I don't…believe them."

Suddenly, I felt Ryder's body against mine. His hands stroked my arms lightly as he leaned close to my ear. "You shouldn't because my heart belongs to you, Jolene. It always has."

He brushed my hair away from my neck and softly placed a kiss there. My breathing had become shallow with anticipation. He whispered, "I'd love to kiss you again."

My breath caught. I turned my head to look into his eyes, and he took the opportunity to capture my mouth. I slowly turned to face him, my hands sliding up his chest to thread through his hair. His hands gripped my waist, and he pulled me even closer. His tongue slipped between my parted lips, and it sent chills all over my body. I became bolder and returned the kiss until we were both breathless. My mind wasn't in control. My body was, and it wanted Ryder.

Suddenly, he pulled away and brushed the hair from my eyes. "I want you, Jolene, but we can't do this right now. How about I show you around." A few moments later, I realized he was right. He was doing this for my own good. I reached out and took his hand and let him lead me through the house.

His house was truly beautiful. His style was very minimal, but it was a house with good bones, as my dad would say. There was a bank of windows in the kitchen that overlooked a good-sized pond.

Ducks were lazily swimming across, and I caught sight of a bunny lurking in the bushes on the edge. Finding my voice, I said, "Ryder, this is so peaceful. I can understand why you fell in love with the place."

He grinned. "It was meant to be. I'd always dreamed of a place just like this."

I just nodded. It was a sanctuary, a perfect place to retreat when you needed to get away from the world. We walked down to the pond, and he showed me the rowboat hidden in the reeds.

"One of these days I'm going to get this boat out and teach you how to catch some fish."

I smiled. "Promise?"

He looked at me with surprise. "Really? I was kidding. I can't imagine you fishing."

"What? I used to fish with my dad. He always put the worm on and took the fish off but I was good at holding the fishing pole!"

He laughed out loud. "Okay, when I go fishing, I'll invite you to come hold the fishing pole. It's a date."

His phone rang and after a quick conversation, he said, "Mason's ready. Follow me." He seemed hesitant to have to take me back. He growled and pushed past me mumbling. "Damn him!" was the only part I could make out. When he reached the garage, he grabbed a helmet hanging by his sport bike and tossed it at me. "Here, put that on," he said avoiding eye contact.

I'd never been on a motorcycle before and certainly didn't know how to put on the helmet. I pulled it on and fumbled with the strap for several minutes before he came over to stand in front of me. Tipping my head back with his fingers, he expertly tightened the strap and snapped it closed. For a moment, our eyes met, but then he quickly turned and pulled his own helmet on. He climbed on the bike, and that was when I realized there was only a skinny little seat for me to sit on.

"Um, you've got to be kidding," I said incredulously.

Checking the gauges and putting the key in, he never turned toward me. "Look, Mason took the SUV so we'll have to ride to town on the bike to pick up the truck."

"But, Ryder, that's not a seat!"

Finally, he turned to look at me. "Jolene…this is perfectly safe. I've had plenty of people ride with me. You just have to hold on tight. Can you do that?"

Biting my tongue, I climbed on behind him and leaned in really close. "Where are the handles to hold on to?" I whispered.

"You hang on to me." He took my hands and wrapped them tightly around his waist. "You okay?" He asked glancing back at me. I could only nod.

I could feel my body trembling with anticipation tinged with fear. There also was the incredible sensation of being so close to him. I was conscious of his rock-hard abs under my hands and how they flexed when he moved to start the bike. As the engine roared to life, I instinctively tightened my thighs around his. We slowly rode down the winding driveway to the gate which automatically opened to allow us to leave. He turned out onto the tree lined street, and soon we were speeding toward town.

Chapter 10

Ryder

I wanted efficient workers and that's what I got. Unfortunately, it cut short the time I got to spend with Jolene. When Mason called to tell me everything at the condo was set up, I didn't intend to be short with him, it just came out that way. I could tell he was confused because he'd only been doing his job. The only saving grace was that she had to ride on my bike with me. When she climbed on behind me and wrapped her arms around my waist, I could have ridden forever. Unfortunately, the ride to Jolene's condo wasn't that long and soon we were pulling up behind Mason waiting in the SUV in front of her building. I braced the bike and instructed her how to get off safely but she only sat there quietly.

"Jolene? Did I scare you?" I asked worriedly.

She finally spoke. "Ryder that was one of the most amazing things I've ever done. I've always wondered what it was like and now I know." Tentatively, she climbed from the bike, her hands trailing slowly over my shoulders. "Thank you for taking good care of me."

Mason climbed from the truck and came over to us. "Boss, I've installed a top of the line alarm that will not only call the police but you as well and have secured the condo. I've also checked out the restaurant you'll be going to this evening." He handed me a slip of paper with the alarms codes on it.

I nodded. "Good work. Now, I need you to take my bike back to the office. I'll pick it up later. Joey or Darryl will give you a ride home."

Mason took the helmet from me and strolled over to the bike. After buckling the strap, he fired it up and quickly drove away.

"He doesn't say much, does he?" Jolene said laughing.

I took Jolene by the arm. "That's not his job. Come on, you'd better get dressed for your date." I winced when I realized how sarcastic I'd said the word 'date'.

She pulled her arm from my grasp and huffed, "It's not a date!"

I couldn't resist teasing her. "Whatever. Say what you want but that's what he thinks it is!"

She lightly punched me on the shoulder, and I could see the hint of a smile on her lips.

As we climbed the stairs to her condo, I familiarized myself with the alarm codes. I unlocked the door and entered them to allow us access. My eyes went immediately to the new motion detectors that the security company had installed. One of the many bonuses of being in the personal protection business was I had connections with alarm companies who were more than willing to do a rush job for me.

Jolene took in the new additions as well. "These aren't cameras, are they?" She asked with a sideways glance in my direction. "Surely, you're not going to be spying on me." She was being playful, and I couldn't keep a straight face.

"No, not unless you want me to," I said giving her a sly grin. "I'll probably just stay here or have someone stationed outside the building at all times."

Shaking her head, she rubbed her forehead with her hand. "I can't believe all of this is necessary."

"Jolene, I'm not sure how much of a threat this guy poses and that's why we're going to be here. At least until we figure out who's behind this."

With a sigh, she motioned to the couch. "Well, make yourself at home. I'll be back in a few."

I wandered over to the window and glanced out making note of her neighbor walking his dog. I checked my phone for messages and found that Joey and Darryl had both checked in for the evening. Ryanne was delivered safely to her home, and they were headed back to the office to do some final paperwork. I reminded them to make sure Mason got a lift home and wished them a goodnight. In no time at all, I heard a door open, and I looked up to see Jolene coming from the bedroom. She had her hair pulled up into a twist and was wearing a black one shoulder mini dress. Her black stilettos made her legs look even longer, and the extra height made her eye to eye with me. She was absolutely stunning. "Do you approve?" She asked twirling in front of me.

"No."

Her smile faded. "Really?"

Shaking my head, I walked over to her. "I don't approve because you look so beautiful Marco is going to want you even more."

She smiled. "You're so silly. He will not. This is one of my own designs. Actually it was one of the last designs I did with the House of Rinaldo." A sad expression crossed her face. "I miss Giada so much."

I took her hand in mine. "I'm sure you had no regrets…no words left unsaid."

She wrapped her fingers tightly around mine. "No, she knew how appreciative I was for all she did for me. I just wish I'd had more time with her."

Still holding her hand, I circled my thumb across her skin. "Life's too short," I said looking into her big blue eyes. "We should always say what we are feeling because any day could be our last."

She stepped closer until we were only inches apart, and I watched as she slowly licked her lips. "Is there anything you'd like to say?" Her eyes never left mine.

I opened my mouth to speak but happened to glance up at the clock and realized we needed to get going to pick up Marco for their

7:30 reservation. "We'll have to finish this another time, and I promise we will. Marco will be waiting for you."

With a sigh she pulled her hand from mine. "Well, let's get this over with."

We drove in silence to the hotel where Marco was staying. He was standing by the curb, obviously agitated as evidenced by his frantic pacing back and forth. His eyes narrowed as he noticed us pulling up beside him. "Finally!" He spat. "I have been waiting for five minutes!"

I climbed out and held the door open for him and under my breath, I muttered, "Il divo."

He turned to look at me. "What did you say?" He demanded.

Calmly and with a smile, I said, "Buon giomo. I thought you might appreciate 'good evening' in your own language."

He frowned and mumbled, "Culo."

I laughed. "Yeah, I've been called that a few times…usually jackass though." Scowling, he climbed in. Making sure to shut the door securely, I walked around to the driver's side and climbed in. Much to my surprise, I found Jolene was now seated in the front passenger seat.

"I prefer to sit up here," she called back to a now livid Marco.

"Antonio's, correct?" I asked as I glanced in the mirror trying to hide a smile.

"Si," he growled. He huffed and pretended to focus on the scenery going by. I saw the hint of a smile on Jolene's lips as she turned to look out her window.

When we arrived at the restaurant, I pulled up and let them both out then handed the keys to the valet. Marco was trying to take Jolene into the restaurant but she seemed to be stalling, waiting for me to catch up. As I walked up, he was saying, "Are we not going to be alone, cara mia?"

She glanced over at me before answering. "No, Marco. Ryder is my bodyguard and he goes where I go." As they walked into the restaurant, I couldn't resist giving a fist pump before joining them.

"Shall we?" I asked opening the door for them. Marco glared at me, daggers shooting from his eyes, but I just ignored him. The beaming hostess greeted us, and I noticed that Marco checked her out from head to toe as he stepped forward.

"Rinaldo, party of…three," he said reluctantly.

"Ah, yes. I'm sorry sir. We are only able to seat you in a booth. Your table is ready. We'll bring the champagne as soon as you're seated." She led us to a large round booth tucked in the back. Immediately, I could sense his dilemma. If Jolene sat anywhere but between us, I'd end up sitting next to him, and I could tell that was a no go.

"Excuse me," I said to the hostess. "Could you bring me a chair?"

Jolene looked at me like I was crazy. "Ryder! The booth is plenty big enough for all of us. You don't need a chair!"

Marco rolled his eyes. "Jolene, if wants to sit on a chair, let him. Prego…after you." She stood her ground refusing to sit unless I joined them in the booth. Finally, I waved the chair away and with a smile, she scooted into the booth. I waited for him to sit down before I took my place on the other side of her.

The waiter, who introduced himself as Alexander, brought menus for each of us but I handed mine back. "I won't be dining."

Jolene's mouth fell open. "Ryder…seriously? You've got to eat. I know this is a job, but be real."

Alexander stood by patiently as I debated my next move. I could almost feel Marco's eyes boring into me. I casually threw my arm around the back of the booth which coincidentally was right behind Jolene and sighed. "Okay, only if you insist, Jolene."

She smiled. "I do, and it's my treat."

Marco stiffened. "Bella, I'm treating you to dinner. Are you telling me you're going to pay for his?" The frostiness in his voice was palpable.

Jolene opened her menu and nodded to the waiter. As if on cue, Alexander handed me my menu back, and I started scanning the selections. I quickly decided on ribollita. I'd had it when I'd had leave in Italy and loved it. Alexander returned with a bottle of champagne chilling in a silver bucket. "Would you like your champagne now, Mr. Rinaldo?" He asked as he arranged everything on a small portable table at my side. Reluctantly, Marco nodded as he glared at me.

Alexander poured Marco and Jolene a glass, but I held my hand up when he offered me one. "No, thank you. I need to keep my head clear."

Marco smiled smugly at my refusal. I could only imagine the toast he'd come up with now that it was just the two of them. "Ti amero' per tutta la mia vita," he said holding his glass high.

I fought the urge to roll my eyes. His toast of 'I will love you my whole life' was a bit overdramatic and frankly, ticked me off. Obviously, Jolene understood the toast as well and I saw a flush come to her cheeks. The whole scene was awkward as he held his glass waiting for her to clink their glasses together. Finally, she spoke. "Thank you, Marco. I will always have feelings for you."

I almost laughed out loud. That phrase was most definitely a kiss off, and Marco didn't catch it. He smiled brightly and took a big swig of champagne. He leaned in for a kiss, but she quickly held up her menu effectively blocking him. He looked miffed for a moment but quickly recovered. Mercifully, Alexander came to take our orders, and the moment passed.

We made our selections and then came the awkward silence. Finally, Jolene spoke. "Marco, did you know I actually gave Ryder his name?"

He appeared confused. "Scusi?"

She continued, "You see, I was just a little girl when his mother was pregnant with him. They were trying to think of a name for a boy and I came up with Ryder. It was a character from my favorite movie 'Tangled'."

I laughed. "My mom told me that story. Thank God that was your favorite. Who knows, I might have grown up with the name Nemo or Simba."

She elbowed me. "I was just a little girl but you were the most beautiful baby I'd ever seen with the biggest blue eyes."

Marco's eyes flickered from her to me. "So, you have known each other all of your lives?"

Jolene took another sip from her champagne. "Yes, our families have always been real close. The only time we lost touch was when I was in England and Ryder was deployed."

Marco's eyes appraised me closely. "You were in the military, no?"

"Yes, I was a military police officer. When I got out, I decided to turn my experience into personal security."

He nodded slowly. "Well, then I guess it's a good thing you are protecting *my* Jolene."

Jolene flinched at the possessive tone he'd used. "Marco, please…"

He took her hand and pulled it to his lips. "It's as if we're strangers. We were so close and I threw it away. Tia Giada would be so sad for us."

At the mention of his aunt, I saw tears glisten in Jolene's eyes. He was getting to her. I sat there biting my tongue. This was between them and I had no claim to her even though right now, I felt nauseous watching this unfold in front of me.

Jolene wiped her eyes with her napkin. "Marco, you're so right. Giada would have been so sad…sad that the only nephew she loved as one of her own children would act like a spoiled child when he didn't get everything he wanted." She pulled her hand from his and rested it in her lap. "You walked away from me like I didn't exist. Now after you realized you messed up, you want me to forget everything that happened. I'm sorry but I can't do that."

Marco's jaw clenched. "Is there no forgiveness for me? Am I to suffer for the rest of my life?"

Jolene shook her head. "No, you'll go on and find someone who can share the kind of life you want to live. You need to find someone who treasures material possessions as much as you do. I assure you, it's not me."

He sat back and rubbed his forehead. "Is there nothing I can say?"

She patted his hand. "Let's just leave it as friends and not say anything that we'll regret."

Alexander walked up with our dinner and Jolene said, "I'm so sorry, Alexander. We need to leave. Could you please wrap up our dinner to go?" Marco began to sputter.

"Of course, ma'am. Is everything okay?" He asked with concern.

She smiled sadly. "Yes, I just think this dinner is over. Ryder, could you get the car and could you make arrangements for a cab for Marco?"

Marco was livid. He stood, threw down his napkin and stalked away.

I jumped into action. "I'll be out front waiting for you." By the time the valet pulled the car to the door, Jolene was standing there holding our dinner. Marco was nowhere in sight.

With a smile, I opened the front passenger door and she climbed in.. "Let's go to my place and eat this delicious dinner."

"You got it." I drove to her condo and escorted her upstairs. Once we were inside, she kicked off her heels and headed to her bedroom. I called after her. "I'll unwrap and heat up our food."

"Oh that sounds wonderful," she called out. "I just have to get out of this dress and heels!"

An image of her changing in the next room filled my mind. I had to shake those thoughts. Throwing our food into the oven to warm it, I found her stereo and put on some soft music. A few minutes later, she came out of her room with her hair tumbling around her shoulders, a white tank top hugging her ample curves and some shorts that just barely covered her shapely rear. Her tanned legs totally distracted me for a moment until the aroma of our dinner caught my nose, and I realized I was just seconds from burning our food. She stood on her toes to reach into the cupboard for plates and then into the fridge for a bottle of wine, and I sat back and admired the view. I grabbed the items as she set them on the counter and quickly set places for us at the bar. She grabbed two glasses from a cabinet, and as I uncorked the wine, she dished the food onto our plates. Within a few minutes, we were seated next to each other, our knees touching. I loved being this close to her…almost too much.

She picked up her wine and held it toward me. "Thank you for being my friend and protector."

I picked my wine up and touched my glass to hers. "Always."

Our eyes met and for a moment, I felt the urge to kiss her but her last comment about being her friend was like a barrier between us. As a diversion, I took a sip of my wine and remarked on how excellent it was. The food was delicious as well. We ate in silence for a while, and the only sound was the clinking of our silverware.

The silence was broken by Jolene asking me pointedly, "So, do you think I'm a complete idiot for having been involved with him?"

I was just about to tell her exactly how I felt about her being involved with him when her phone rang. She ignored it at first, waiting for my answer, but finally she glanced at who was calling and she answered.

"Oh, hey, Mom!" She paused, and I could hear a very frantic voice asking if she was okay. "Yes, I'm fine. I know I should have called you but a lot happened really quickly. Did Olivia tell you what happened?" Another pause as her mom chattered away. Finally, she was able to catch a break to jump in. "Well, Ryder's with me now. He's my own personal bodyguard." She gave me a wink as she said it and my heart skipped a beat. "No, I don't think this person would really hurt me but you can never be too careful. There are a lot of nutballs out there in the world today." She took another sip of wine and then a deep breath. "Mom, I know you're worried but I'm not going to let this crazy person run me out of my home. I appreciate the invite to stay there but Ryder's already got my place all secured and plus he's keeping an eye on me 24/7."

I got up and gathered our dishes and started to load the dishwasher. She watched me with a crooked smile rolling her eyes occasionally at something her mom said. "No, I don't plan on cancelling the show. I'm sure Ryder has a brilliant security plan already put together."

I smiled. She knew me well. We'd already had a basic security plan for the show, but with recent events, I'd have to change the assignments for the day. Now, I'd need to be in charge of Jolene with Darryl as backup and Joey and Mason were going to be handling Ryanne.

I had to admit. Jolene's assessment of Mason was spot on. From the day he'd come in for his interview, he hadn't spoken more than a handful of words at a time. His credentials were impeccable, and I felt confident he was a good fit for the team. He had a background in law enforcement having worked for the Los Angeles Police Department but after having been injured during a standoff with a drug-crazed suspect, his marriage fell apart and to start fresh, he'd given up that part of his life and returned to his hometown.

The mention of my name brought me back to Jolene's conversation. "I'll tell Ryder you said that," she said with a grin. "Goodnight, Mom, and tell Dad not to worry."

She hung up and I couldn't hold back my curiosity. "What did your mom say?"

"She said for you to take good care of me." She slid off the barstool and walked over to where I was standing in the kitchen. She took my hand and linked it with hers. "Will you take good care of me?" She asked, batting her eyelashes.

My heart started hammering in my chest. "What exactly do you need?" I managed to croak.

"I need you," she simply said. Taking my hand, she led me to the couch then she reached over to turn off the lamp. The only light was from the moonlight streaming through the blinds. She sat down and pulled me down to sit beside her. "I feel so safe with you," she murmured as she tucked her legs under her and leaned against me. I wrapped my arm around her, and she pulled herself even closer.

Her head was resting on my shoulder, her hair spilling over my arm. The faint fragrance of vanilla drifted up, and I couldn't resist pressing my lips to her hair.

She lifted her head from my shoulder, and her eyes focused directly on my mouth. I swallowed hard as she turned to kiss the side of my neck. "Mmm," she murmured against my skin, and I felt my pulse begin to race. She began to feather kisses toward my jaw until she was just one kiss away from my mouth. Her eyes met mine, and she hesitated. "Can I kiss you?" She whispered.

I nodded as she molded herself against me, the heat of her body searing me wherever it touched. My hands wound themselves into the soft waves of her hair, and I pulled her to me. As our lips touched, I felt her tongue trace my bottom lip before her teeth gently nipped it. "You have the softest lips," she whispered. My hands moved down her back to cup her waist, allowing me to pull her against me more tightly. She gasped then snaked her hands under my shirt stroking my stomach. "Oh God," she moaned. "You're gorgeous!"

Using both hands, she lifted my shirt pulling it completely over my head. She dropped it onto the floor then her hands started exploring my chest, her fingers outlining my abs. I tugged at the hem of her shirt, pulled it over her head, then dropped it next to mine. She was wearing a frilly off-white bra made of satin and lace. I ran my fingers across the silky fabric then stroked her soft skin. I captured her sweet mouth again and pressed her to me, our bare skin now touching, the heat between us growing with each second. She pulled away, her hands trailing over my bare chest. She stood and shimmied out of those tiny shorts, and I was delighted to see she had panties to match her bra. Beautiful was the only word that came to mind. She moved to straddle me, and we kissed as our hands explored each other's bodies until we were both breathless. I was poised to unhook her bra when the front door bell rang. "Are you expecting anyone?" I said quietly.

"No," she whispered. "Plus, they would have to call the intercom to get in." She scrambled off of my lap. "I'll go see."

Keeping my voice low, I said, "No! Let me look!" I grabbed my gun and made my way through the darkened room to the door. After checking the peephole, I cracked the door open slightly.

"What the hell?" Jolene gasped.

At the threshold was a bouquet of dead roses with a note. It read *I can get to you, anytime, anywhere.*"

Jolene's eyes were wide with fear. Slamming the door shut and locking it, I wrapped my arms around her and pulled her close. She was trembling and tears were pooling in her eyes. "Shh, I've got you," I assured her. "Thank God I was here."

She stiffened in my arms. "Oh, God." A sob escaped from her lips. "Ryder, I'm so scared. What does he want?"

Gently kissing the top of her head, I murmured against her forehead, "I don't know, but I'm going to find out and stop this."

Chapter 11

Jolene

With my attempt at seduction totally ruined, there was nothing left to do but go to bed, alone. Ryder had insisted on sleeping on the couch to keep an eye on things. I blushed thinking about how brazen I'd been. I rested my flaming cheek against the cool pillow and fell into an exhausted sleep.

The sun streaming through the cracks in my blinds woke me and after a good stretch, I crawled from the bed. After a refreshing shower, I wrapped my head in a towel and padded into the kitchen. Ryder was folding his blanket and as he looked up, a huge smile lit up his face. "Hey sunshine," he said walking over to wrap me in his arms. "How'd you sleep?"

"Like a brick that drools," I said laughing. "I was fine knowing you were out here keeping watch. How did you sleep?"

He smiled. "I didn't."

I frowned. "You stayed awake all night?"

He nodded and with a devilish grin said, "Yeah, the snoring kept me up."

I smacked him on the arm. "You can kiss my—" I was interrupted by my phone. It was Olivia.

"Hey, Liv!"

"What in the hell is going on, Jolene? I've been trying to call you ever since you left the office yesterday and finally Mom called and told me she'd talked to you. Is everything okay or was that the 'lie to Mom to keep her calm' story?"

Checking my phone, I saw it was on vibrate and there were several missed calls and voicemails. "Oh gosh, Liv, I had my phone on silent. Actually, there was an incident here last night but thank goodness Ryder was here with me."

Olivia sighed. "Jolene, when you become famous, it doesn't matter what you do. People have fantasies about celebs and they believe they're true. This guy may have seen you in a magazine…who knows. The point is, he's targeted you and that's the problem. Do you want me to cancel the show? There's still time and Maxine would totally understand."

"No!" I blurted. "I'm not going to let this crazy person run my life. Ryder assures me that we can do the show without being in danger and that's what we need to do. Can you call Ryanne and make sure she's okay and still willing to do it? I've got to finish getting ready and then I'll head to the office."

"I'm on it," she said. "Be safe."

I hung up the phone and turned to Ryder, who was sitting at the bar finishing a bowl of cereal. "Olivia's worried about the show. Should I be?"

He shook his head. "My crew can handle it and Ryanne's not going to have Gage with her. Rusty's parents will be in town and he'll be spending time with them. Between the four of us, we can watch you two."

I leaned on the counter. "I'm putting my trust in you." I gave him as confident a smile as I could but inside I was shaken.

I'd just come out of the bedroom after throwing on a pair of yoga pants and a tank top when I heard the intercom. Ryder jumped to his feet, answering the door in seconds. As he spoke, a huge smile came to his face. A few moments later, he whipped the door open and immediately I saw why he was smiling. It was Lucinda!

"Hey, babe!" She said as I rushed to give her a hug. "I was just passing through…"

"Lucinda!" I squealed. "I can't believe it's you!" I took in my bestie's amazingly unique style and smiled. She was dressed in a black and white color block mini with black stilettos. Her accessories were chunky black and white bracelets and large matching hoop earrings. She looked absolutely gorgeous!

Ryder held out his arms to her. "Hey beautiful," he said as he wrapped her into a tight hug. "How the hell have you been?"

When she stepped back she looked back and forth between us. Her eyes traveled up and down Ryder's body. "Is this fit bloke really Ryder?" She then looked at me and with brows raised said, "Um, did I interrupt anything? A snog session perhaps?"

My face reddened. "No, nothing going on here," I said, suddenly feeling the need to fluff the pillows on the couch. I risked a glance at Lucinda and could tell what she was thinking. Why else would Ryder be over here first thing in the morning having breakfast with me. She gave me a knowing smile. "So, tell me what are you doing here? I'd have thought you'd be busy making wedding plans!"

As soon as the words came out of my mouth, her expression grew somber. Ryder must have seen it too because he glanced at me and said, "Hey, since we have a few minutes before we need to leave for the office, I'm going to make some calls. I'll be down in the car. You girls catch up."

He gave Lucinda another quick hug then left us alone. "Sweetie, what's wrong?"

She took a deep breath and sighed, her bottom lip trembling. "Trevor and I broke up."

I took her by the hands and led her to the couch. "Sit and tell me everything."

She sniffled then began. "The last time we talked, I was almost certain he was going to propose. We took the Eurostar to Paris and he'd booked us into a brilliant hotel overlooking the Eiffel Tower. I'd packed all of my sexy undies and was all set. He'd seemed a bit preoccupied on the train but I figured he was nervous like I was. There was champagne in the room and he immediately poured some and chugged his like a sailor. He asked me to sit, which I did then he proceeded to tell me that he loved me but wasn't in love with me anymore. He said that he'd always promised me a trip to Paris and he'd kept that promise but it was also a goodbye."

I listened in stunned silence. Tears were spilling down her cheeks as she continued. "When I asked what I'd done wrong, he told me it wasn't me, it was him. He said he'd been at a party and met someone. She's an art student and just nineteen. He assured me it had never gotten physical but he wanted it to but he respected me too much to cheat on me so he ended our relationship so he could begin one with her."

"Lucinda, I'm speechless. Trevor? He adored you! I really can't believe he told you that way either. It's just awful!"

She nodded. "Yeah, I was totally taken by surprise. I cried my eyes out and screamed at him to get out which he did, suitcase in hand. I stayed the weekend by myself and drowned my sorrows in French wine. When I got back to London, he'd moved out of our flat and was gone. I sat there and started to wallow in my own pity then decided I needed a change and the first place I thought of was here. I've got a room at the Ballentyne and am headed there now but wanted to stop here first."

"Lucinda! You are NOT staying at a hotel! You have to stay with me!"

She laughed as she wiped the tears from her cheeks. "Babe, I can't do that. It's obvious you've already got company and I need to be near you but also need to get my head together. Plus, fashion week starts next month so I have to be back by then."

I blushed. "Really, there's nothing going on."

She laughed. "Yet?"

"It's not like that. Well, I can't say I haven't tried but we got interrupted by my stalker."

"Your wha--?"

"My stalker. It seems I'm the target of some obsessed nut and until Ryder figures out who it is, he's got me under his protection 24/7."

Her eyes grew wide. "Has he threatened you?"

I nodded. "Yeah, he's sent me packages and letters and even some dead flowers at my door. It's scary and I guess the only way I can deal with this without freaking out is to make light of it."

"Well, I for one am glad Ryder's taking care of you. It's obvious he cares about you."

I stared at her. "Just how would you know that?"

She smiled. "He told me. Years ago when he came to visit, we spent a lot of time talking about you. He's loved you for a long time."

I scoffed. "Loved me? That's called a crush, Lucinda."

She shook her head. "Nope, it's called knowing who your heart belongs to and setting your mind on making it happen. I thought I had something like that…not anymore." A tear slipped down her cheek.

"I'm so sorry. It'll get better, I promise. Let's change the subject. How's the new job?" I asked as I handed her a tissue.

"It's good," she said as her gaze shifted away from mine. I immediately sensed something was wrong there, too.

"Hey," I said patting her on the shoulder. "You want to talk about it?"

Another sigh. "Well, there's another designer there who absolutely hates me. She's constantly insulting my work and it's already getting old. Fazon is her name and she thinks she's God's gift, if you know what I mean."

"Fazon?" I scoffed.

"Yeah, she insists on being called by that name too. I don't know if she has a last name, to be honest."

I put my arm around her shoulders and gave her a hug. "Well, my dear, you are going to forget all about Trevor, Fazon and anything else that's bothering you. You're in my town now and we're going to have a blast."

A knock came at the door. "Jolene? It's time to head to the office," Ryder called through the door.

"We'll be out in a minute," I shouted before turning to Lucinda. "We'll drop you at the hotel so you can check in and unpack and rest, I'll call you and we'll get together. How's that sound?"

She smiled. "Sounds fantastic. Let's go."

We joined Ryder in the car along with Lucinda's luggage which we took from the cab that had been waiting for her downstairs. "I can't believe you didn't tell me you had a car waiting!" I admonished her. "They cost money!"

As we pulled from the curb, she laughed. "Honestly, he did look a bit put out when we came and took my things. He'd been flirting with me all the way from the airport. He was kinda hot! The money wasn't a problem though. My new job pays pretty well."

Ryder looked up in the rearview mirror. "Where are you staying, Lucinda?"

"Um, I booked a suite at the Ballentyne," she said looking at her planner.

"Whoo, you must be doing pretty well. That's a four-star!" He said giving her a big smile.

"It's my first holiday in the US, I want only the best!" She grasped my hand and gave it a squeeze. "I'm so happy to be here and see where you came from!"

We pulled up in front of the hotel, and the bellhop came dashing to the door. Lucinda climbed out, and I noticed him checking her out right away. Lucinda's red hair and dark green eyes were a striking combination, and her unique style made her stand out. Ryder unloaded her bags and I went in with her to make sure she got checked in with no problems. At the elevator, I gave her a hug, and I told her I'd talk to her later.

As I climbed into the front seat of the truck, Ryder turned and smiled. "Jolene, you look so beautiful. Being happy suits you." I blushed and smiled.

As Ryder and I arrived at the office building, I noticed a few paparazzi hanging around outside. "Do they have nothing better to do?" I groaned.

Ryder laughed. "You're somebody. How's it feel?"

I scrunched up my nose. "Not great, to be honest."

He turned to me and with a serious expression said, "Well, when we get out, do exactly as I say. Any of these low-lifes could be your creeper."

He parked at the curb and as he opened my door, he took me by the hand. "Stay right next to me and head for the door. Don't look at anyone, just look straight ahead. I'm doing the looking."

He placed his hand on the small of my back and quickly led me through the crowd that had quickly gathered around the truck just that few moments we'd sat there. "Jolene! Jolene!" I heard someone call.

"Miss Anderson! Is this guy servicing *you* now?" Another one yelled. Ryder grabbed my hand and pulled me forward.

"Are you carrying his love child? You *do* look pregnant!" I heard from someone beside me.

When I heard that, I immediately stopped and as a result, my arm almost got pulled out of the socket by Ryder. A balding man with a camera was standing there with a grin. "Did I hit a nerve?" He said leering at me.

Before I could respond, Ryder wrapped his arm around my waist and he physically lifted me from the ground and carried me into the building. "RYDER! What are you doing?" I yelled as he put me down in the lobby.

"Jolene, look, they're saying that stuff to get pictures that they'll use to make up a story. If you attack, they get exactly what they want!"

Drake was standing in the lobby watching the door to make sure nobody followed us. "Are you okay, Miss Anderson?" He asked with concern. "I tried to have the cops run them off earlier but that didn't work. The cops said as long as they weren't on our property, they really couldn't do anything to them."

I took a deep breath to calm myself. "Thank you, Drake. I just don't see what they find so fascinating about me."

He shock his head. "Miss Anderson, I'm sorry but I totally see it. You're a beautiful, talented woman and they are just trying to find out more about you." When I blushed, he stammered. "I—I'm sorry, I didn't mean to embarrass you."

Ryder smiled. "I agree with you, Drake. She is an amazing woman. She just doesn't see what we do." Now blushing furiously, I let him lead me to the elevator. As the doors shut and we began to go to our floor, he backed me against the wall, and his fingertips trailed across my cheek. "I'm sorry but I've wanted to do this ever since we got interrupted last night." He leaned into me, and I held my breath. Our lips touched and I felt tingles all over my body, like tiny electric shocks. His hands wrapped around my waist pulling me to him. I parted my lips with a sigh and felt his tongue dart out to stroke my bottom lip. My heart was beating wildly in my chest, and my hands snaked their way up to clutch the front of his shirt. Our bodies pressed together, and I felt his hand slide under my shirt to touch my bare skin. I arched toward him wanting him closer. "Jolene," he groaned. "You make me crazy."

I tried to speak but couldn't. My knees felt so weak, and I couldn't breathe. He feathered kisses down my neck, and I closed my eyes. It was as if the world stood still.

Suddenly, the elevator slowed and he pulled away. He gave me one last kiss on the forehead before the doors opened. I was thankful he made me stay back as he secured the area because I needed that extra moment to gather my wits. I'd never felt such intense desire before in my life, and it scared me. What I'd had with Marco was nothing compared to what I was feeling for Ryder. With my pulse racing, I stepped from the elevator, and he once again placed his hand on the small of my back. "You okay?" He whispered with a devilish grin as we walked into the office.

I was about to answer when I heard Olivia say, "It's about time you two showed up. I've been worried sick!" She was standing in the middle of the office, hands on her hips and tapping her foot furiously. "Ryder Brisson, you may be protecting her but you have to promise that you'll do a better job at keeping me in the loop." She turned her attention to me. "You owe me big time for handling Mom and Dad. You're welcome."

"I'm sorry, Olivia," Ryder said as his eyes scanned the room. "It was really a spur of the moment thing. I can't have too many people knowing Jolene's schedule. Someone may inadvertently give away her location to the stalker and that's no good."

She glared at him. "Do you honestly think I'm that dumb?"

He walked over and rested his hand on her shoulder. In a calm, soothing voice, he said, "No. You're her sister and I know you wouldn't do anything that could put her in danger. All I'm saying is that people desperate for information will lurk around those who would know and overhear things. It's just better to keep things simple."

I could see her anger slowly subside. "Okay, you're right. He could be the window washer for all we know."

Ryder nodded. "Yeah, could be."

We were interrupted by the door opening as Ryanne and Joey came in. She came rushing over to me. "Jolene, are you okay? Joey told me there'd been a break-in and some crazy threats!"

I nodded as she hugged me. "Yes, some moron has decided I'm his obsession for the time being. Hopefully he'll realize I'm pretty boring."

She looked at me with a puzzled expression. "You? Boring? Hardly. You're exactly the type of person the public wants more of. You're young, beautiful and single. Unfortunately, you're also the perfect target for a loner with your picture plastered all over his bedroom walls. Believe me, I've had my share of those and it wasn't fun. That had a lot to do with my decision to back away from public life when I was pregnant with Gage. The paps were camped out trying to get pictures of me going to the hospital to have him and more importantly, pictures of him. One nurse got fired because she snuck a camera in the nursery at the hospital. She'd been paid a lot of money to get pictures of Gage but luckily, Rusty walked in on her and was able to get security to get the camera away from her. She later admitted that one of the tabloids had put her up to it but she also defended her actions by telling us her kid needed college money. It was upsetting and an eye opener to think that people you think you can trust are the ones who'll stab you in the back for a quick buck. Rusty and I decided then and there to share the pictures of Gage with 'Superstar' magazine and that took the bounty off of our heads."

Just the thought of someone chasing a pregnant Ryanne or even little Gage made me nauseous. Ryder must have seen my queasy expression because he sat me down and grabbed a cup of water. "Here drink this," he said, kneeling in front of me. "It's going to be fine, I promise. Do you trust me?"

I nodded. I did trust him. I trusted him completely. With a deep, cleansing breath I said, "I'm not going to let this stop me. Let's get busy. We've got a show to plan!"

Chapter 12

Ryder

As Jolene and Ryanne went back into the conference room to do some final preparations for the show, I got my team together to go over strategies for the event itself. I assumed since it was to be held in a boutique that we wouldn't have a lot of area to cover, but then I pulled the venue up on the computer, and my heart sank. Maxine's Closet was a 20,000 square foot building on the outskirts of Charlotte. That was a lot of square feet to cover with just the four of us. We found the original building information, and I was thrilled to see that ABC Designs had been the architects when it was built years ago. ABC Designs was the firm owned by my mom along with Jolene's parents.

When I was younger, I asked my mom why she and my dad didn't work together as they were both architects and she said at the end of the day, they could both leave their projects at the office and not have to worry with any of that at home. It made their marriage work.

I called my mom to see if she could help.

"Hey, sweetie!"

"Hey, Mom! Are you busy?"

"I always have time for you, Ryder. What's up?" She asked.

"I need to go over the plans for Maxine's Closet. Jolene's fashion show is going to be there and I'm doing security."

"Ah, we loved that project. Tell me what you need and I can email you the blueprints."

"Mom, you're a lifesaver!"

We spent about an hour going over the layout. She pointed out any vulnerable parts of the building such as fire exits, outside doors, etc. By the time we'd finished going over it, I had a clear plan, and it was going to be workable with my crew.

Suddenly, I heard a commotion in the hallway and leapt to my feet. I yanked open the door to my office and found Marco standing toe to toe with Olivia. "What's going on?" I asked moving next to her.

Olivia was livid. "This piece of crap won't get the hint. He is trying to see Jolene and I'm not going to let that happen." Suddenly, we heard a shriek from inside Jolene's office. Marco charged for the door, but I easily pushed him out of the way. Jolene, who was standing by her desk, was holding a picture. She was visibly shaken, and Ryanne was trying to comfort her.

"What is it, Jolene?" I asked. She was as white as a ghost.

She handed it to me as if in a daze. I looked at it and could immediately understand why she had freaked out.

It was a photo taken of us the night before as we arrived at her condo. It had been taken with a high-powered lens from somewhere across the street. My face had been obliterated by a black marker scrawled across it. Marco grabbed Jolene's arm tightly and glaring at me he snarled, "You are making danger for her! This maniac is upset with YOU!" He hissed.

Returning the glare, I growled menacingly, "Get your hands off of her."

He obviously got the message because he released her but then moved between us and said to her, "After this show is finito, you will find another security firm."

Jolene shook her head. "No, I won't. You don't own me, Marco."

He backed off and slowly walked to the door then turned and snarled, "This isn't over."

Pulling Jolene into my arms, I stroked her hair. She was trembling but soon calmed down. "Ryder, what do we do now?"

After taking a deep breath, I said, "You said it, the show must go on."

Things calmed down eventually, but everyone was on edge. I sent Mason home with Ryanne and kept Darryl and Joey close by. Despite the extra security at Jolene's, I still didn't feel comfortable with her staying there. It was too accessible so when she finished for the day, I informed her she was going home with me.

She was gathering her things from her office, and I could tell my decision wasn't going over very well. "Ryder, I don't see why. I'll admit I was unnerved when those flowers showed up at my door but you'd be there."

Darryl was in the outer office so I shut the door giving us some privacy. "Look, I'm not psychic. I don't know who's doing this to you and until I have more information, I'm going to minimize the risk. The police fingerprinted the box you got the other day and came up with some prints but nothing in the database. I'm giving them the picture you got today and probably will get the same results. You mean too much to me to put you in danger."

She pursed her lips and narrowed her eyes. "Well, will you at least let me pack some clothes? I don't think you'll have anything in my size." Her lips curled into a smile.

I stepped toward her and gently tucked a stray curl behind her ear. "Be sure to pack some of your lacy goodies," I whispered in her ear.

A flush crept across her cheeks. "Um, I never go anywhere without them," she said giving me a sexy smile.

Darryl knocked on the door to let us know the truck was waiting downstairs. "We'll have to pick this conversation up later," I said with a grin.

I asked the guys to escort us down and then gave them the night off. As we passed through the lobby, I saw Kris was working the desk in the lobby, and I gave him a quick wave on my way out but then I heard him call my name. As he rushed over, I told the guys to take Jolene to the truck. He seemed very nervous as he pulled me aside. "Uh, Mr. Brisson. I need to tell you something."

I glanced at my watch hoping this wouldn't take long. "Sure, Kris. What's up?"

He glanced around then said in a hushed voice, "I think I may know who you're looking for."

Confused, I said, "Excuse me?"

He appeared agitated, and I was starting to get an alarm bell going off in my head. He whispered, "I heard someone's been bothering Miss Anderson. I have information that you may find useful."

Now he had my interest. "Okay, tell me what you know."

"Okay, the other night, I came in and Drake was on the phone. I heard him mention her name and when he saw me come in, he looked startled and hung up immediately. There was no goodbye or anything…just hung up. It looked really suspicious."

His information didn't seem earth-shattering so far. "Okay, so he said her name then hung up. Is that it?"

He screwed up his face. "No! I'm no idiot. Let me finish! The next day, I was at work and I got ink all over my jacket. I called Drake to ask him if he had an extra one in his locker that I could borrow and he said yes. When I opened his locker, I saw a folder in the very back with Miss Anderson's name on it. I was curious and probably shouldn't have done it but I looked inside and found pictures of her. Lots of them along with a map to her house. I put everything back in the folder just like it was and shoved it back in the locker right before Drake came in. He looked really upset probably because he realized what I'd find when I went to get the jacket. I pretended I didn't see anything and I must've been convincing because he relaxed right away. I went to the front desk and a few minutes later, he left. When I clocked out for the night, I peeked in the locker again and the folder was gone."

Drake, the doorman. I never would have put him on my list of possible suspects but this was a definite lead. The objective now was to keep an eye on him without letting him know. "Thanks Kris. You've been a big help. If you see anything else, let me know."

"Will do, Mr. Brisson. I really like Miss Anderson and don't want anything to happen to her."

I smiled and clapped him on the shoulder. "Me too."

Jolene was sitting in the front seat with a puzzled expression on her face. When I climbed in, she glanced over. "You okay?" She asked as she lightly touched my arm.

I gave a quick nod. "Yeah." I cranked the truck and headed to her place. She obviously felt uncomfortable there because as soon as she walked in, she drew all the curtains and closed the blinds. She quickly packed a bag and within minutes we were headed out.

As we drove to my house, she said, "Ryder, I need to call Lucinda. She's going to wonder what happened to me."

"Sure, you can call her but don't tell her where you are. The less she knows, the better…for her."

She nodded slowly. "Right…I didn't think about that." She called her room, and she answered right away.

"Lucinda, it's me!" She said with a smile.

I could hear Lucinda's cheerful voice on the other end.

Jolene glanced at me then said, "Well, there's been some crazy stuff going on lately. I can't really go into it but to make a long story short, I won't be able to hang out with you this evening, like I'd hoped."

She sounded so disappointed that I said in a hushed voice, "Tell her I'll have someone pick her up in the morning and bring her to your office. You guys can hang out there."

Her face brightened immediately. "Hey, Ryder's going to have one of his guys pick you up and you can come spend the day with me."

She nodded then said, "Sure, I think ten will be fine." She looked at me and lifted her eyebrows for confirmation.

I nodded yes and they happily finalized their plans.

As we pulled into my driveway, I quickly scanned the area, entered the code and when the gate swung open, drove up to the house.

Chapter 13

Jolene

As we drove up to Ryder's house, all I could think about was being alone with him again. The night before, if we hadn't been interrupted, I'd been ready and willing to sleep with him. Now, after some thought, I realized that wasn't the best idea. Tonight, I was going to be spending the night with him, and I didn't know if I'd be able to keep my hands to myself.

As soon as we walked in, he carried my bag up to one of the guest rooms and right away, I felt the pang of rejection. Secretly, I'd been hoping he'd carry it into his room, and I could play the 'you think I'm that easy?' card but he never gave me the chance. He showed me where I could put my clothes and showed me a huge bathroom with a massive garden tub. "This is all yours," he said with a sweep of his arm. "I've got a shower in my bathroom. I'm going to let you settle in while I whip us up some dinner."

The tub looked so inviting that after he walked out, I decided to take a nice long soak in it. I unpacked a few things then grabbed my robe along with my iPod with earbuds and started to run some water in the tub. I was delighted to find some bubble bath in the cupboard and after adding it, the sweet aroma of gardenias filled the room.

I piled my hair on top of my head and then after slipping out of my clothes, I gingerly stepped into the tub. The water was a little hotter than I expected, and I let out a little yelp as I did. Slowly, I lowered myself into the bubbles with a sigh. I popped the earbuds in my ears, closed my eyes and lost myself in the music.

I heard the doors close behind me, and I pushed the button for the ground floor. Out of the corner of my eye, I noticed someone standing against the back wall of the elevator. The numbers began to flash as the elevator began to descend. Suddenly, it ground to a halt, and the lights went out. Nervously, I said out loud, "This sucks!"

There was silence from my fellow passenger.

I could feel sweat beading on my forehead as the reality of being trapped in this elevator began to set in.

Despite the pitch black, I could sense the person moved closer to me. I took a step closer to the front, my hands desperately searching for the emergency button but instead found a blank wall.

My heart began to race, my breath coming out in short bursts. 'Calm yourself,' I said over and over in my head, but it wasn't helping. Why wasn't the person trapped with me saying anything?

I decided to try again. My voice shaking, I said softly, "Are you okay or are you scared like me?"

Suddenly, I felt someone press against me, hot breath against my neck.

"Please stop," I stammered. "What do you want?"

"I want you, Jolene."

The stalker! He was with me in the elevator. Tears sprung to my eyes as the desperation of the situation came crashing around me. I needed help…I needed Ryder!

Summoning all my strength, I managed to find my voice, "RYDER! RYDER!" I screamed.

Faintly, I heard him respond. He had to be on the other side of the door.

"Ryder! I'm here! Help me!" I cried as I pounded on the cold steel door. He pounded back, and I knew he was close but not close enough to help me.

I felt the hair stand up on the back of my neck as a hand gripped my arm and held on tight. I squeezed my eyes closed tightly, wishing I was anywhere but here.

Again I heard Ryder call, "Jolene!"

"Jolene!" My eyes popped open to find Ryder standing over the tub, his hand gripping my arm. I looked around and realized I was still in his house, in the tub, and then it hit me. I was naked!

"What happened?" I gasped trying to cover myself.

Turning his head to minimize any further embarrassment, Ryder handed me a towel which I used as I climbed out of the lukewarm water. "Apparently, you fell asleep and I came up to let you know I had dinner ready and I heard you calling out my name. I knocked on the door but you didn't answer. You sounded so scared that I threw the door open and found you here in the tub. Are you okay?"

Clutching the towel with shaking hands, I nodded. "Yeah, I guess I'm more stressed than I realized."

He pulled me into his arms and gently kissed the top of my head. "It's okay, I've got you."

I looked up and I pressed my lips to his neck. He groaned, his throat rumbling against my mouth. He sighed and then said, "Jolene, as much as I want you, I can't. Keeping you safe is what I need to keep my focus on. When this is all over, believe me, I'm going to show you how much I want you.

My face crimson with embarrassment from his rejection, I backed away and said, "Okay, well, I need some privacy, please."

His eyes were sad as he nodded. "I understand. I'll be downstairs." He backed away and at the door turned to go but hesitated, shook his head slightly, then walked out the door.

To say things were awkward the rest of the evening was an understatement. Rejection was crushing and regardless of the reason, it hurt just the same. When I joined Ryder for dinner, I tried to put on a smile and act like nothing was wrong but inside, the feelings I'd had after my breakup with Marco resurfaced. I went to bed early and once in bed, lay awake thinking of everything that had happened in the last month. My heart had been broken and yet here I was, willing to throw myself on someone else.

We fell into a routine in the next few weeks, and the time passed quickly. I stayed at Ryder's despite my protests that I needed to go home. He assigned Darryl to drive us in and had him shadow me at the office all day. It felt weird, as if he didn't trust himself alone with me. When we were at home, he seemed to be constantly working, and so I would wander around the house or venture out in the yard but always within sight of the house. One time, I felt as if someone was watching me, and I glanced up at his bedroom window to find him there. He didn't conceal himself. He just watched me.

During this time, I was so thankful there was no contact from the crazy creep but that dream still came back on occasion and I'd wake up holding onto my pillow, tears staining my cheeks. I stayed busy preparing for the show and with Lucinda's help, we had an amazing collection to present.

The night before the show, I was doing some last minute alterations in my room. Olivia and Lucinda had come over to help me. I was so happy to have them with me, especially since it had been so awkward with Ryder. Lucinda had been an invaluable help to me with the clothes, and Olivia had been busy lining up the models. Everything was coming together beautifully.

Earlier in the day, on the way home from the office, Darryl had stopped to let me pick up my mail. The girls were chatting away about whether or not to bring some of the leather belts as accessories so I picked up my mail to see what I'd gotten. One letter was from a reporter who worked for 'Celebrity' magazine begging for an interview. The news reporters had been making up stories to go along with the pictures they managed to get whenever I arrived or left the office. One picture was from that memorable morning when Ryder had tossed me over his shoulder and carried me kicking and screaming into the building. The headline read "She Likes It Rough" and it proceeded to tell its readers that I was totally into S&M and bondage. It also printed a picture of Marco looking pretty darn happy at a nearby nightclub with a young woman on his lap. The story went on to speculate when I would get tired of my new man candy and go back to the love of my life. I tore that letter in half and tossed it in the trash.

Another letter was sealed in a pink envelope with no return address. I slid my finger into the flap and ripped it open. Inside was a picture of my mom and dad's house along with a note telling me that no one was safe and soon we'd be together, forever. I felt the blood drain from my face and Olivia, who'd been doing the last minute checklist, noticed immediately. "Jolene, are you okay?" I slumped down onto the bed still clutching the letter. "Ryder!" She called downstairs. "Come here! I think our boy has done it again."

Ryder came sprinting up the stairs and rushed into the room. Seeing my stricken face, he pried the picture from my hand and scanned it quickly. "Son of a bitch," he said under his breath. "I'll be right back."

Lucinda and Olivia both tried to comfort me but my security bubble had been popped once again. After a few minutes, Ryder came back upstairs. "Ladies, I think it's best for you both to stay the night and we'll be able to leave first thing in the morning to head to the show. This is becoming a logistics nightmare and having you both here will make things a lot easier."

Chapter 14

Ryder

Darryl checked in and gave me an update that everything was secure. I'd left him and Joey with the girls, so I could meet Mason and do a final run-through on the location. For the past few weeks, we'd been finalizing our plans and tomorrow was the big day. When I'd called Ms. Abernathy, she'd been more than cooperative and assured us that she'd have someone there to let us in. The first time I'd actually seen it, I found it was the one of the most spacious boutiques I'd ever seen. Ms. Abernathy, who'd insisted I call her Maxine, showed up in person to give us keys, so we could arrive early and prepare. Tonight, expecting wall-to-wall clothing and racks, I found instead a large room with all of the merchandise against the walls and the center of the room was filled with comfortable chairs, which flanked a large runway. We quickly located the exits and any vulnerable points that someone who was a serious threat could infiltrate.

When I felt we had everything laid out, Mason and I went to the house to relieve the guys. After giving them the detailed instructions, I encouraged them to get rested and to meet us at the boutique at eleven. Maxine had closed the store for the day in anticipation of her big event, and I was thankful she had. Mason volunteered to keep an eye outside for a while, so I went upstairs to Jolene's room.

Jolene's eyes lit up when she saw me. "Ryder! I—we missed you!" She gave me a friendly hug. "How did it go?"

She and Lucinda were going over some sketches as Olivia sat watching the television. I sat down and laid out the plans for the show.

"Do you think he'll show up?" She asked as she looked over everything.

With a shrug, I said, "My motto is 'better be safe than sorry'."

She nodded. "I guess you're right. We don't know who we're dealing with."

My conversation with Kris came to mind. I'd been doing some checking into Drake's background but had come up with nothing incriminating in his background.

"I have a feeling it's someone who knows your schedule because they're close to you."

She frowned. "I can't believe a friend would do that to me."

"Money's a powerful thing and will make even the closest friends turn on each other," Olivia said looking over my shoulder.

Jolene sighed. "It's like you can't trust anyone anymore. Especially if money's involved. But why threaten me? Why ask me to get rid of you and Marco?"

I shrugged. "I don't know yet, but I'm going to find out. I know one thing for certain, he's on my radar and if he shows up tomorrow, his ass is mine."

"Do you think we'll be okay tomorrow?" She asked, worry creasing her brow.

"My guys are top professionals. They've been briefed and will be on the alert for anything strange."

Olivia and Lucinda who were both yawning, said goodnight and headed to their rooms.

Jolene's face was filled with worry, so I placed my hand on her shoulder and kneaded her tight neck muscles.

"Ahh," she groaned. "That feels amazing."

I sat behind her on the bed so I could work both shoulders. She moaned as I circled my thumbs on the back of her neck. "God, your hands are amazing." I could feel the tension leaving her body and soon she was leaning back against my chest. I pulled her hair aside and began massaging her neck. Suddenly, she stiffened. "I think you'd better go."

Her reaction was all my fault. The night I'd found her in the tub, I'd wanted to make love to her but in my heart, I knew that having her at my house was for her protection, not for her to be in my bed.

Slowly, I got up from the bed and after giving her shoulder a final squeeze, I left her. I couldn't sleep. Closing my eyes, I lay there remembering how good it felt to hold her in my arms. Her kisses were so soft, and I longed to have her in my bed, but I knew I had to be patient.

I must've finally dozed off because the alarm woke me. I crawled out of bed and into the shower. Feeling refreshed, I wrapped myself in a towel and crept out into the hallway to head to my room, and I ran right into Jolene. "Hey beautiful," I said as we passed in the hall. "Come downstairs when you're ready. I'll make some coffee. You like cream and sugar, right?"

She gave me a sad smile. "Yes, you remembered that?"

"I remember going with you to the coffee shop and you always made me get it for you. Not that I minded because it gave me a chance to spend time with you."

Placing her hand on my arm, she gave it a squeeze. "You've always been so good to me."

I placed my fingertips under her chin and tilted her head to bring her gaze to mine. "You make it easy."

Lucinda came out of her room, so I quickly pulled my hand away and headed to my room. "Oy, don't stop on my account," she said laughing.

I shut my door and quickly dressed and went downstairs to find Olivia and Lucinda were having breakfast. As I walked in, Lucinda's eyes met mine and she gave me a smile.

She dug around in the fridge and found some orange juice. "So, what's the story with Darryl?" She asked as she flopped into a chair. "Is he married, single, or just not into crazy chicks like me."

I poured myself some coffee, leaned against the counter and laughed. "His name is Darryl Yancy. He's single, he played college football, and from what I found out on the internet, was really good at it but didn't want to turn pro. He also used to be a bodyguard for some of the professional football players. I don't know what his type is but I can tell you that a man would be a fool not to be into someone like you."

She grinned. "Thanks for the compliment. I may just see what happens with the mysterious Mr. Yancy." Turning to Olivia, she said with a laugh, "I need to learn about American football."

We sat around and chatted for a bit and then Jolene came into the room and for me, the world stood still. She was gorgeous dressed in a black strapless sundress paired with a simple strand of black pearls. Her hair was pulled up into a bun revealing a matching pair of tiny black pearl earrings. I quickly made her a cup of coffee, and as I handed it to her, she smiled. "Thank you," she said softly.

"Whoo! Jolene, you look amazing!" Lucinda said with a whistle.

She grinned. "It's one of my new designs. They'll be in Maxine's Closet within the month. Maxine approved all of the designs for manufacture and they're being expedited to her stores."

"Then I'll be the first in line to get one," she said.

I checked the time and realized we needed to get going soon. "Ladies, we'll be heading out in about thirty minutes." They finished up their drinks and went back upstairs to gather their things.

I decided everyone should ride separately for safety's sake. We left as a motorcade with Darryl in the lead with Lucinda, Jolene and myself in the middle, and Joey and Olivia bringing up the rear. Mason was escorting Ryanne and her family and was due to meet us there. When we arrived, the parking lot was quiet making our entrance uneventful. Maxine was waiting at the rear door to let us in, and she escorted us to the dressing areas which were now blocked off to the front. I took a quick look through the curtains and could see the runway and the chairs all set up. We met up with the models and makeup artists who'd been hired for the event.

Within moments of arriving, everyone was bustling around handling the final touches. My team and I blended into the shadows and it gave me the opportunity to watch Jolene at work. I'd teased her about 'making clothes', but watching her work, I was flat out amazed. The models were gorgeous, and she went to each one and chose the exact makeup to showcase their natural beauty. They gushed over the clothes, and many begged to be able to keep the samples they were wearing. She graciously assured them that she'd make sure they all received one of their favorite pieces as a thank you for participating.

"Jolene? I need you for a minute," Olivia called out. Ryanne had just come from the dressing area and needed accessories. "I need to see what accessories you want to put on her," Olivia said holding up several possible jewelry pieces. Quickly pairing something up with each outfit, she went off to help someone else with finishing touches. Time flew by and suddenly it was time for the show. Maxine came back to see how everything looked and was thrilled. She gushed about the entire collection and also informed Jolene that they had a full house. Members of the media were also in attendance to cover Ryanne's first show in several years. I could see Jolene's anxiety level start to rise but then her eyes met mine across the room. I walked over to her, put my arms around her and whispered, "You've got this." She was trembling, and I knew she was barely holding it together.

Lucinda came up, tapped me on the shoulder to scoot me out of the way, and also gave her a hug. "Babe, you're a star. I knew it from the first day we met. I'm lucky to have such a beautiful and talented bestie." Tears filled her eyes. "I love you, honey."

I radioed to my crew to get into position. I gave her a quick kiss on the cheek. "I'll be close by. You won't see us but we'll be there."

With a nod, I signaled to Olivia that everyone was ready. I could hear Maxine welcoming the crowd to a rousing round of applause. The soundtrack Jolene had chosen was fast paced electronic music and the models were moving to the beat even before going out onstage.

Ryanne was the first out and Jolene double-checked to make sure everything was perfect before she pulled back the curtain. She gave her a hug then with a deep breath, she calmly turned and headed out. The applause was instantaneous and as each model went out it never dwindled. She was so focused on the show that she was startled to see Ryanne was back for her first change. Olivia and Lucinda helped her quickly slip out of one dress and into another. Everything was going like clockwork. The crowd was enthusiastically cheering throughout the show. Olivia came up behind her and threw her arm across my shoulder. "Last one, sis. Time for you to make your grand entrance."

This was a part of the show I'd been concerned about. She was going to be standing in front of a crowd without me right next to her, and I felt helpless. I stood behind the curtain and heard Maxine say, "Ladies and Gentlemen, the talented designer of today's fashions and Charlotte's own, Jolene Anderson!"

Stepping onto the runway, she made her way between the models who flanked the stage. Her parents were in the front row along with mine, and I could hear them cheering for her as she gave them a little wave. Her brother, Ethan, was seated beside Carter, and they were both whistling loudly as they pumped their fists in the air. Maxine was standing at the end of the runway signaling for her to join her. She handed her the microphone and said, "Please say a few words?"

Her hand was shaking as she took the microphone. "Hey everyone! Thanks for coming today! I'm so thrilled to be teaming up with Maxine's Closet for the launch of my collection. All of the designs you've seen here today will be available exclusively for purchase in every one of her boutiques within the month. I'd like to say a special thank you to Maxine, Ryanne Charles and my beautiful models, my sister Olivia, my best friend Lucinda, my parents and family and my dear friends who have supported me through this entire project." She was just about to hand over the microphone when she blurted one last thing, "Ryder...thank you for everything."

Cheers came from the audience as she handed the microphone back to Maxine. People came rushing to the stage, and she was suddenly surrounded by a sea of exuberant well-wishers. This was not good. I rushed to get to her but was hampered by the models who were still on the stage. I saw a hooded man grab her arm and yank her to him roughly. Radioing the guys to check the perimeter for a man in a black hoodie, I pushed my way through the crowd, and just as I reached her, the man quickly jumped from the stage and disappeared into the crowd.

"Are you okay?" I touched her and she jumped as if shocked. "What just happened, Jolene?!"

Wild-eyed, she spun around trying to see where he'd gone. "H--he was here, he grabbed me!" She stammered.

"Did he hurt you?" I asked wrapping her into my arms.

"No, he just grabbed me," she said her body trembling uncontrollably.

"Did he threaten you?" I asked as I scanned the crowd for any sign of him.

"No…he said he wanted me and would have me." She paused and then softly said, "He said he'd kill the bodyguard if he had to."

A moment later, the last person I wanted to see strode onto the runway. "What is going on? Who was that man?" Marco demanded.

I ignored him but he persisted. "I saw that man grab Jolene! I want to know where her security was!"

"I'm okay, Marco," Jolene managed to say. "He didn't hurt me."

Marco was furious. "I knew I shouldn't have left you with him!" He spat out. "He is an idiota!" Jolene just stood there in shock. Marco continued, "She is no longer under your care! I will take her to my hotel for safety. I will take care of my woman."

Scoffing, I shook my head. "You're going to protect her? How do you think you can do that?"

Marco clutched her arm. "I'm a man and I know what's best for her. I should have never left her." He placed his fingers under her chin and gently lifted her face to his. "Cara mia. Let me take you home with me. I will take care of you like I did before. Per favore."

Dazed, she turned to me, and I knew right then she was going to go with him. I pleaded with her. "Jolene, you know I'm more capable of protecting you. You know I care about you more than anything."

Tears filled her eyes as she said, "Ryder, I think it's best that I stay with Marco, for both of our sakes."

"What do you mean, for both of our sakes?"

Tears welled in her eyes. She turned to Marco. "Could you give me a second?" Marco reluctantly stepped away but not before kissing her hand. He stepped away but not out of sight.

"Ryder, I—"

"Jolene, I need to know what you mean." I reached for her, but she took a step back.

"I think we're getting too close. My feelings are all mixed up and I can't think straight." She bit her lip as a single tear rolled down her face.

"Too close? Jolene, why won't you let this happen between us? I know you feel something for me, I can tell when I kiss you. Can't you tell I'm in love with you?"

More tears fell as she shook my head. "No, Ryder. You've always had a crush on me. I think the dream is better than the reality. I shouldn't have let things get as far as they did and now I realize that it wasn't right to take advantage of you."

I was incredulous. "Take advantage of me? You are the only woman I've ever loved. Please don't push me away. Please."

She backed further away. "Ryder," she sobbed. "Please don't—"

"Jolene, this isn't the way it has to be. Don't let *him* convince you he can protect you!"

Marco strode over. "Basta! Enough! Cara mia, I'm moving to a new hotel now. You will be safe there. This crazy man will not know where to look for you." It was obvious she wasn't thinking straight. Marco led her to the door where his car was waiting. She looked over her shoulder at me and mouthed 'I'm sorry'. Marco helped her into the car, the door closed and they drove away.

"Are you serious?" I turned to see an irate Olivia standing next to me. "Are you just going to let her leave with that Italian douche?"

I sighed. "Liv, she's a grown woman and right now, she's confused and it's clouding her judgment. No matter what I say right now, she's not hearing it."

"Well, I don't trust him as far as I could throw his Ferragamo loafers. He's got an agenda, I just know it." She tapped her foot furiously. "So, are you going find out where they are?"

I nodded and grinned. "You bet your ass, I am."

Gathering my crew together, I explained the latest events and planned our next move. Darryl escorted Lucinda back to her hotel and Ryanne left with Rusty's security. Mason and Joey came with me.

Before she left, Lucinda pulled me aside. "I'll be honest with you, Ryder. I liked Marco at first but after he did what he did…I'm sorry but he's a plank. Give Jolene some time and his true colors will show once again. Have patience, babe," she said.

She was right. If I tried to force myself into the situation, Jolene would just back further away. I needed to let her find out for herself. I promised Lucinda I'd check in with her later, and then I found my dad. No matter what I did in my life, my dad was my go-to guy when I really needed advice, and this was definitely one of those times. He and my mom were still milling around wondering what had happened.

"Hey son! What in the hell is going on?"

"Dad, first I've got something important to tell you that will help you understand the rest of the story." I paused to take a deep breath. "You know Jolene's been having some trouble with a stalker. Well, she hired me to take care of her but somehow today, the creep slipped by me and made a serious move that could have been deadly."

He nodded. "That makes sense. The look on your face when you bolted past us onto the stage was dead serious."

"That's because I'm in love with her." He looked at me with surprise. I continued, "I know, it's hard to believe but I've felt this way for a very long time."

He laughed. "Ryder, I believe you. When you were little you had a crush on her and that was cute but when I saw you two together just now, I saw something much deeper going on. I even said something to your mother. She and I have been hoping that you two would get together."

My mouth fell open. "You knew? Was it that obvious?"

He nodded. "You were as transparent as glass. Son, when your mom and I met, I looked at her the same way, like she was the most amazing woman on the planet. That's what love will do to you."

I shook my head and laughed. "Damn, I wonder if she saw it."

He nodded. "I guarantee it. So, what's going on with you now? Have you told her how you feel?"

I rolled my eyes. "That's where it gets complicated. There's another guy…"

"Oh hell," he said with a groan. "An ex?"

I nodded. "Yes, Marco…an ex who threw her away and now has come back into her life. He's manipulating her and I don't know what to do about it."

His eyes grew wide. "Is that who she left with?"

I sighed. "Yes, she let Marco talk her into it and I don't know where they are. She told me that it was better for the both of us if she went with him. Right now she's in his hotel suite somewhere. I don't know who this stalker is but if he's watching her, no doubt he'll know where she is now but I don't have a clue."

He studied me for a moment. "Son, your job is a tough one. When it's personal, it makes it even harder. I know this is kind of obvious but why don't you just text her and ask her to tell you where she is, for safety's sake."

"Dad, sometimes you need a kick in the head with the obvious," I said giving him a hug. "Thanks, I love you."

"I love you too, son. I'll explain what happened to the rest of the family. Get to work."

I headed back to the office but as soon as I walked in, I noticed Drake lurking in the lobby. A plan popped into my head as soon as I saw him. "Hey, man!" I said throwing up my hand in greeting. "How're things going?"

He looked startled and also wary. "Um, good Mr. Brisson. How are you?"

I smiled. "Great! I'm going to do some work in the office then take a quick shower because, my man, I have a hot date tonight!"

His eyes narrowed. "H—hot date? Anybody I know?"

Giving him a cheesy grin, I said, "Maybe…let's just say she's a famous fashion designer and she's drop-dead gorgeous. Do you know anyone that fits that description?"

He frowned then gave me a weak laugh. "Um, I think so?" I could see his hands were trembling.

I kept pushing his buttons. "Yep, she called me and I'm meeting her over at the hotel. I'm going to pick her up, wine and dine her and then…who knows."

His face turned a sickly shade of green. "Sounds like you have a great evening planned." He swallowed hard, and I saw a bead of sweat trickle down the side of his face.

I gave him an exaggerated wink. "Great evening? I hope it turns into a great morning too, if you know what I mean." Satisfied that I'd done enough, I walked to the elevator and when he turned his back I slipped into the janitorial closet and let the elevator go. Quietly, I crept out and could hear him talking loudly on the phone.

"He just walked through here and told me he's got a date with her!" He said angrily. "How is that possible?"

He listened for a moment then said, "I am doing everything I can! What else can I do?"

More listening and finally, "Look, I'm NOT giving any money back. I did the job and I'm keeping it. Besides, I've already bought a new Mustang with the money."

The plot thickened. He was working with someone and they had money.

Drake rambled on about his new car for a few minutes and then said, "Can you slip away and meet me? I've got more pictures to give you. I promise I won't stalk her!" He laughed and it made me sick to my stomach. Jolene was caught in the middle of these two sickos and had no idea. "Okay, I'll meet you as soon as Kris comes in."

He hung up and dabbed the sweat from his forehead. I snuck down the hallway and up the stairs to the next floor where I caught the elevator up to my office. A light was on in Jolene's office so I knocked and Olivia came to the door. She was working late, putting everything away from the show. I asked her to please do me a favor and call down to the lobby and find out when Kris was due to come on duty. When she hung up, she told me he was supposed to be on the desk in thirty minutes. I went into my office and texted Jolene.

I respect your decision and won't interfere but I'd appreciate knowing where you are. I do care.

A couple of minutes later she responded.

I'm sorry if I acted weird. My feelings are so mixed up right now and I appreciate you giving me space. I'm in room 803 at the Westin. My own room.

My heart leapt at the last line. She wasn't staying with him so I still had a chance and if I could just get to her room without detection, I could try to get her to listen to me.

Thanks for still trusting me. I'm here for you. Always xx

I took the elevator back down to the lobby and saw Kris at the desk with his back to me. I walked out without a word and headed toward the towering Westin.

Chapter 15

Jolene

As I lay my phone on the nightstand, I heard a knock at my door. "Tesoro, it's me, Marco." I walked to the door and checked the peephole before opening it to let him in.

"What do you want? And STOP calling me that!" I asked with more than a hint of irritation. I really hadn't wanted to leave with him and especially not to end up stuck in a hotel room. My emotions had confused me, and now I was definitely paying for it.

He touched my hair and I flinched, which he immediately noticed. "Why do you pull away? I only want to make you happy," he said frowning. When I didn't respond, he walked over to my phone and picked it up. "Have you heard from him?" He sneered.

"No, I haven't." I tried to get my phone away from him but he held it out of my reach. Thankfully, I'd deleted the message from Ryder. "Marco, I made a mistake coming here because it appears you've taken it the wrong way."

Eyes narrowed, he scowled. "Are you saying you wish to leave?"

I nodded slowly. "That's exactly what I'm saying. I should have listened to Ryder."

His lips curled into a smirk. "And what exactly did he say? Did he tell you he loved you?"

His contempt only served to fuel my courage. "As a matter of fact, he has told me that."

He stepped closer to me, and I could see the tightness in his jaw. "Did he warn you about me?"

Reflexively, I took a step back. "No, he didn't. And I wouldn't have believed it if he had." I felt goose bumps rise on my arms. There was a look in his eyes I'd never seen before, a very dark look. Then, just as quickly, it was gone.

"Well, cara mia, I would never hurt you," he said with a brilliant smile. " I love you! I've just come to tell you that I've made all the plans for our flight to Genoa and once we're there, we can pick a date for our wedding. I've even made arrangements to pick up your English friend, Lucinda. You will want her by your side, yes?"

My jaw dropped. "Wedding? Are you insane? I never said I'd marry you!"

He reached out to grip my arm tightly, his tone menacing. "Jolene, I have friends watching those you love. Friends who could do things to your precious Ryder. If you don't marry me, it will be bad for all of them."

My heart was hammering in my chest. "You wouldn't!" I spat. "Why would you want me if I don't love you?"

His face morphed again, this time into an evil grin. "I need you," he said simply.

"Need me for what?" I asked trying to pull my arm away but he held fast and even tightened his grip.

"I need you to help rebuild the House of Rinaldo. You see, I have a love of gambling and beautiful women and unfortunately, it has depleted my inheritance to dangerous levels. With your reputation, we can be successful again. I will have my money and, when I feel the urge, you waiting in my bed as well. You loved me once, you can grow to love me again."

I felt sick to my stomach. "You're twisted and sick, Marco."

He smiled and nodded. "This is true. But I'll be rich and that's all that matters." He turned and started toward the door. "Listen carefully, Jolene. I have someone guarding the door so don't even think you can leave to go anywhere. I have an important meeting and I'll return soon. This will give you a taste of what's to come." He pulled me roughly to him, wrapping his arms around me to force his lips to mine in a bruising kiss. His tongue was trying to pry my lips apart, but I fought him. I managed to free my hand, and as he finally broke the kiss, I slapped him as hard as I could on the face. His eyes narrowed as he massaged his now red cheek. "Soon, you will come to your senses, or else. Ciao!" He walked out and as he did, I ran to the door and threw the deadbolt to keep him out. I tried to see out of the peephole, but his thug was leaning against the door blocking it.

The tears threatened to come but I fought them, instead focusing on my next move. I walked to the nightstand to get my phone and realized it was missing. The bastard had taken it! I picked up the hotel phone and was greeted by a message saying the phone was blocked from use. Damn him! I threw myself onto the bed, sobbing into my pillow.

About fifteen minutes later, I was startled by a loud thump against the door followed by a firm knock. Cautiously, I crept to the peephole and was relieved to see Ryder's face. I tore open the door and threw myself into his arms. He quickly backed me into the room and over his shoulder, I saw the feet of someone laying in the hallway. "What did you do?" I gasped as he turned to retrieve the prone figure by dragging him into my room, then he shut the door.

"Don't worry, I didn't hurt him. He's just going to sleep for a while. He will have a hell of a headache when he wakes up though." He gathered me into his arms, and I melted against him. "Jolene, are you okay?" He asked kissing the top of my head.

I looked up into his eyes and blinked back another wave of tears. "I am now. Ryder, he's crazy. He thinks he's going to take me to Genoa and marry me. He needs money and apparently, I'm his cash cow." My lip began to quiver. "He threatened to have someone hurt you if I didn't go along with it," I confessed.

Ryder gazed at me and brushed my hair from my eyes. "I would never have let that happen. I love you, remember?"

I gave him a sad smile. "I should have listened to you." A single tear dropped from my lashes onto my cheek. He quickly but gently brushed it away with his thumb.

"There's still time, but we have to hurry. Grab your things, I'm taking you to my house. He won't find you there."

I looked around and realized that the only thing I had with me was my phone, and it was gone. "I don't have anything." Linking my hand in his, I said, "Let's go."

Before we left the room, Ryder made sure my 'guard' was still out, then led me down the hall to the elevator. As it rose, we could hear voices coming from the elevator shaft and one of them was most definitely Marco's. We backed away from the door and quickly found the door to the stairs. As we descended, I prayed Marco wouldn't go to my room for a while and find me gone. Ryder's truck was still in the valet lane thanks to an apparently healthy tip, and we jumped in and pulled away without any sign of pursuit.

As we rode along, our hands found each other and linked together tightly. Being with him, I felt so safe. So much had happened that my mind needed to shut down. I dozed off but right before I did, I heard Ryder talking to Lucinda.

"I'll have Darryl take you somewhere safe. I wouldn't put it past Marco to try to use you to get to Jolene."

What seemed like just a moment later, Ryder's hand eased from mine waking me up instantly. "Shh, it's okay, we're at my house," he said softly. "It'll just take me a minute to reset my gate code just in case someone who has it felt like sharing it with our Italian friend."

Nodding, I yawned and stretched as I watched him lean out to take care of the alarm. The gates swung open, and we drove up to the house. I moved to open the door, and he shook his head no. "I've got it," he called out as he came around to my side. The door swung open, and he held his hand out for me to step out. Not letting me go, he led me into the house and switched on a few lights. He armed the alarms for the perimeter before pouring me a glass of wine. "Here, drink this. It'll relax you."

I smiled. "Ryder, I don't need anything to relax me. I feel so safe when I'm with you."

He took me by the hand and led me to the couch. "Sit and I'll be right back. I need to make a few more phone calls to make sure I have everything covered."

I sat down on the soft leather and curled my legs under me, then quickly finished my wine, which was excellent. The only sound was the ticking of the grandfather clock and the hum of the air conditioning. The wine relaxed me, so I lay my head against the throw pillows, closed my eyes and quickly drifted back off to sleep.

"Jolene?" A soft whisper in my ear woke me. My eyes slowly cracked open to find Ryder kneeling at the side of the couch, his face inches from mine. When my eyes finally focused, I saw that he was smiling. "Hey beautiful," he said softly.

"Hey you," I whispered back.

"You okay?" He brushed the hair from my eyes.

"Yeah, I think so. So much has happened lately, I just crashed. How long was I out?"

He glanced at the clock. "About two hours to be exact. I came in a couple of times to check on you but you were fast asleep. I figured you might be hungry."

I shook my head. "No, not really. This is just so stressful, I wish I could just get my mind off of everything, to just escape."

"Sounds good," he said with a smile. "Where would you go?"

I thought for a moment. "If I could go anywhere, I'd go to Ft. Lauderdale." He smiled a knowing smile. "Do you remember the vacation we took with our families? That was my favorite."

He nodded. "Yeah, you took your friend, Kathy, and all you wanted to do was chase boys up and down the beach. The only good thing was you never caught any."

I laughed. "Well, to be honest, Kathy was the one doing the chasing. I was shy about talking to boys. You were the only one I could talk to. One thing I do remember was going out on the charter boat, and of course, I got seasick. You were right there holding my hand, and my hair. Come to think of it, you've always been there for me whenever I've needed you."

He cradled my face in his palm. "Yeah, I guess I always looked out for you because...well, I think you know why." His eyes locked onto mine for a moment then he looked away.

"Ryder, please look at me. I guess I've always known you cared about me and when we were younger, the age thing was always on my mind. But now, I look at you so differently. You're a man who's served this country. You've gone to dangerous places not knowing if you were ever coming back. I can't put into words how proud I am of you and what you've accomplished. When I came back from England, you were one of the first people I wanted to see. I was so disappointed that you weren't there. When you showed up at my door, frankly, I was blown away. I hate to admit it but in my mind, you were dangerous to my heart and I vowed to try to steer clear of you."

He looked puzzled. "Dangerous?"

"Yes, definitely dangerous. I could see myself falling for you hard. I'd just been through the breakup with Marco and didn't think I had any feelings left to give anyone but the minute I saw you, I knew I could easily lose my heart."

His fingertips softly touched my face. "I have a confession to make. I never stopped thinking about you. The guys at Bragg all knew about you and I told them that one day, I'd make you fall in love with me. Of course, they harassed the hell out of me for being a lovesick wussy but that was okay because I still clung to the dream."

Our eyes met, and he leaned in closer. He hesitated slightly so I slid my hand around his neck and pulled him to me. Our lips met and just like before, it was as if an electric shock went through my body. A moan escaped my lips, and I felt him scoot closer to slide his hand around my waist pulling me against him. My fingers traced his shoulders, his muscles taut under my touch. He pulled away from my lips and began to feather kisses down my neck. "Mmm, that feels so good," I whimpered.

His mouth pressed soft kisses at the hollow of my throat sending chills all over me. I gasped but the sound was captured by his lips. My cheeks flushed with desire, my body was on fire. I guided him up onto the couch where he settled beside me, our legs entwined. "You're so much better than the dream," he said softly into my ear.

Those words captured my heart. "I want you," I whispered. He propped himself on his elbow and gazed into my eyes.

His lips brushed mine then suddenly, his phone rang. "Don't move. I need to see who that is. Stay right where you are." He gave me another quick peck on the lips then quickly hopped up.

"Brisson," he answered while glancing over at me. He paused and said, "Okay, keep her with you until I tell you otherwise." Another pause then, "If you feel your place is secure enough, that's fine with me." He hung up and turned back to me. "Lucinda's safe with Darryl. He's taking her to his apartment."

I chuckled. "I know this is probably not the time to say this, but I'd love to be a fly on the wall in that apartment. Cool, quiet Darryl alone with crazy, wild Lucinda? I'd pay to see that."

He came back over to sit on the edge of the couch. "You know, Darryl's really not that shy. He's just very professional when he's on the job. Who knows, they may hit it off." He leaned in close, his nose touching mine. "Now, where were we?"

Snaking my fingers into his hair, I whispered, "Right here." I gently nipped his bottom lip with my teeth. He groaned and I couldn't resist whispering, "Do you want me to stop?"

He took a shuddering breath and shook his head. "You stop and I'll die right here." His phone rang again. "Damn it! What now?" He angrily pushed the button to answer.

"Brisson!" Instantly, his face clouded over. "What in the hell do you want?" I immediately sat up at the change in his tone. "Look, you don't have any claim over her. She doesn't want you!" He looked at me before shaking his head. "No, you bastard. You are NOT talking to her." He listened for a moment then hung up.

"That was Marco, wasn't it?" He didn't answer but I knew it was. "Wha—what did he want?" I whispered.

He leaned down and touched my face. "I'm sorry, Jolene. I'll be right back."

He left me hanging so I called out, "Ryder, you have to tell me what he said!" There was nothing but silence.

I pulled my knees to my chest. My thoughts were a jumbled mess, and I couldn't think. What could he do? Who would he try to get to next? My hands grew clammy as I thought of the people I loved being in danger. I grabbed Ryder's house phone and dialed my mom. She answered on the first ring. "Hello?" Her voice was shaky.

"Mom? It's me."

"Jolene! Oh thank God!" She gasped. "We've been sick with worry. Justin told us what happened at the show. Are you with Marco? Honey, are you safe?"

"No, I'm not with Marco and yes, I'm safe with Ryder. I called to make sure you guys are okay. Marco's gone crazy and I'm afraid of what he might do."

"We're okay. We'll get the family together and go to the cabin your father and I used to go to in the mountains. We've got Ethan with us but we haven't been able to get Olivia to answer her phone."

My stomach did a somersault. "Olivia?" I said breathlessly. "Mom, did you try the office?"

"Yes, of course I did. I've also tried her cell constantly for the last couple of hours but it keeps going straight to voicemail. Do you think she's okay?"

Oh no…Olivia. An easy target for Marco. "Mom, I don't know but please keep trying. I'm going to let Ryder know. Stay close to your phone so we can let you know if we find out anything. Also, if you hear from Olivia, call Ryder's phone."

My mom let out a little sob. "Please stay safe."

Tears welled in my eyes. "I will, Mom. I love you."

"We love you too."

Ryder came back into the room, his face somber. "I've got some bad news. Olivia's missing," he said softly.

I collapsed back onto the couch. "I was afraid you were going to say that. My mom said she hasn't been able to get in touch with her. Ryder, you have to tell me what Marco said. Did he say something about her?"

"Jolene, I don't know how to say this." His face was tortured, and I knew it was bad. "I thought there's no way he'd be that sick and twisted. He said that the pain you felt when you lost Giada was nothing compared to what you would feel when you lost your beautiful sister." I gasped and started to cry. He continued, "I called Joey and sent him to your office. He found her purse there and her phone was in it."

I could barely speak. "Did he say what he wants?" A sob escaped from my lips.

"Marco said you'd know what to do."

Tears flowed freely down my cheeks. "If I have to make a choice, then I only have one option. I'd do anything for Olivia and if that means trading myself for her, then I'll do it. I hope he'll let her go and that I'll be able to get away from him eventually on my own."

His expression was thunderous. "Do you honestly believe I'm going to let you go with him?"

"Ryder, what else can I do? He could kill her." My voice broke, and I buried my face in my hands.

He knelt in front of me and pulled my hands to his lips. "Baby, I'll get her back but I'm also not letting you out of my sight. I need to get the guys together to put together a plan, immediately. Marco told me you had one hour to call him at this number with your answer," he said dropping a piece of paper with a phone number scribbled on it onto the table.

His phone rang, and I saw it was a call from Mason. He went into his office leaving me alone with my fear. Every scenario in my head of a confrontation with Marco ended with someone getting hurt or even killed. In my mind, the only possible way to handle this was to meet Marco alone and convince him to let Olivia go. If Ryder was anywhere nearby, he'd hurt her, I knew that now. I walked to the office door and could hear Ryder talking. His car keys were on the side table, so I quietly grabbed them along with the slip of paper and headed out the door.

I cranked the SUV and rolled out the driveway with the lights off so he wouldn't see me leave. I wasn't sure if the alarm would be triggered from my leaving but it was a chance I had to take. The gate opened automatically and as soon as I hit the main road, I floored it. I used the phone in the truck to call and Marco answered on the first ring.

"Ah, you do not disappoint," he growled. "I promise, cara mia, you will not regret your decision."

"Cut the crap, Marco. Where's Olivia?" I snapped. "You better not hurt her! I want you to promise you'll let her go."

His voice grew angry. "Fine! I promise but only if you promise to marry me."

Fighting nausea, I managed to say, "I still don't understand why you want me so badly, but I will. Just let her go."

"Bueno. Come to the airport. I have my private plane out on the runway ready to leave. You go to the gate and my man will meet you and lead you to me. I do have one condition, however, if Ryder is anywhere near you, I'll kill her. I mean it."

My heart was beating wildly as I turned onto the road toward the airport. "He's not with me, I promise."

Chapter 16

Ryder

I finished my phone calls to the crew. They were prepared to converge on a moment's notice wherever Marco designated as the meeting place. When I walked back into the den, Jolene wasn't there.

"Jolene?" I called. "Honey, are you upstairs?" Taking two steps at a time, I went to the second floor, quickly scanning the rooms. She was nowhere to be found. I happened to look out the front window and saw my truck was missing.

"Oh God, Jolene, you didn't!" I yelled as I bounded down the stairs. Throwing open the front door, I dashed down the steps to scan the driveway. She was long gone.

I called our building and asked for Drake.

"Mr. Brisson? Is—is something wrong?"

"Actually, Drake, there is something terribly wrong. We have reason to believe Miss Anderson's in danger and we were hoping you could help us out."

"Wh—why would you think I would know anything?" He stammered.

"Well, we know that someone was stalking her and threatening her so of course we'll be turning over anything she received to the FBI for fingerprinting. We also will need any surveillance video from the last few days in case anyone suspicious was lurking around the area."

"Fingerprints?" He squeaked. "Can they really do that?"

"Oh yes, they can even get DNA from the envelope if the person licked it. But time is of the essence. If you know of anything that can help us, we need to know now."

"Well," he said, softly. "I think I know who may be involved. It was that guy Marco. He paid me to scare her…but I never thought he'd hurt her!"

"So, are you saying you were involved in this?" I growled.

"Yes, I was," he said softly. "The money was hard to turn down. I've always wanted a new car and with the money from him…along with the money from the tabloids, I was able to buy it."

"You were the informant too?!" I asked, my voice rising. Taking a deep breath, I calmed myself. "You were feeding information to the paparazzi?"

"Yes, I gave them some of the pictures that I took for Marco and gave them information…some of it real, some made up. They paid me pretty well. Do you think she's okay?" He asked softly.

"I have no idea. Do you know where he might be?" I asked, my patience wearing thin.

"No, but I do know he had a private plane at the airport. Does that help you?"

"Yes, it does. Thank you. We'll be in touch." I hung up then it hit me. I cursed myself for not thinking of it sooner. "OnStar! My truck has it!"

I called the number and informed the operator that my truck had been taken and I needed to know where it was. She told me that it was in the vicinity of the Charlotte/Douglas airport. "Do you want me to inform the driver that the police are being called?"

"No, I'm in law enforcement," I answered quickly. "I'll take care of this. Just keep me informed every five minutes of its location. I'll be on my motorcycle so please call me." I gave her the number.

"Yes, sir. I'll be glad to call you with updated information." I put my Bluetooth in my ear and called Mason and Darryl. "Head to the airport, I'll meet you in front of the main terminal."

Twenty minutes later, I was pulling up in front of the airport. Mason and Darryl were waiting when I arrived and right behind me, Joey pulled in. I'd received an update that the truck was parked in the private departure area of the airport. "Let's hope Marco's plane is still here. Mason, call the airport police and stop it any way you can."

Mason called, found out it was still on the ground and informed them there was a private security issue involving the plane. He asked that they contact the tower to delay their departure. The air traffic controller told us they had already been approved to taxi to the runway for takeoff. I sped to the location he gave us, I rounded the corner of the hanger slowly just in time to see Marco push Olivia down the steps before they retracted and the door closed.   Luckily, he hadn't seen me. My heart sank, however, when I saw my SUV sitting nearby, empty. Olivia was running toward the terminal, glancing back over her shoulder as she ran. I messaged Darryl and told him to get her picked up.

Now it was time to get Jolene. The rest of my team moved in. Joey came riding up on a stolen tug, wearing maintenance coveralls over his street clothes. He drove the cart directly into the path of the plane and stopped. The pilot stopped immediately, and was gesturing wildly at him. Joey just threw up his hands and stayed put. The diversion allowed me to quickly station myself near the door. Moments later, the door opened, the steps came down, and Marco emerged.

I sprung out from behind the steps catching him by surprise. Startled, he spun to try to run back into the plane but I tackled him, slamming him face first into the door frame with a loud thud. As I kept my arms wrapped tightly around his legs, he began kicking trying to break free. He tried to claw at my face so I took his ankle and twisted it causing him to shriek in pain. He swung his fist making contact with my jaw causing me to lose my grip momentarily. Pulling his foot free, he kicked at my face but I was able to grab his ankle again and twist until I heard a loud snap.

He screamed in pain but managed to get his hand on the door frame and pull himself inside. I was right behind him. By the time I got into the plane, he was trying to lunge behind the seat. I grabbed him by the back of his shirt and pulled him back. That was when I saw the gun. He whipped it around, his eyes wild. Thinking quickly, I struck him on the wrist trying to dislodge the gun and with my free hand, I swung for his face. The first punch glanced off his chin and I was relieved to see the gun drop to the floor. After quickly kicking the gun out of his reach, I delivered a second punch to his abdomen which doubled him over.

"You...ass..." Marco wheezed.

I punched him again, this time in the face, and heard the sound of his teeth click together. He swayed, but I still held him by the front of his shirt. I pulled my arm back prepared to give him another blow, but his knees buckled, blood dripping from the corner of his mouth.

"Basta! Basta!" He gasped. He held up his hand in surrender. I released his shirt and he fell to the floor, wincing in pain.

Hearing someone behind me, I turned to find Mason and Joey staring down Marco. "Good job, Boss," Joey said with a smile.

Giving him a nod, I said, "I knocked his gun loose, be sure to secure it." I then turned my attention to finding Jolene. I searched the seats, working my way to the back of the plane, where I found a locked door. "Where's the key?" I called to a dazed Marco, who was being pulled from the floor and tossed into a seat.

With trembling hands, he fumbled in his pocket and handed a key to Mason who tossed it to me. I quickly unlocked it and froze when I opened the door. Jolene was lying on the bed, her eyes closed.

"Jolene!" I knelt beside her and took her hand in mine. She wasn't responding. "What did you do to her, you bastard?" I yelled.

Marco, who was wiping the blood from his face with the back of his hand, whimpered, "I gave her something to make her sleep."

I turned my attention back to Jolene. "Baby, wake up. Jolene, it's me, Ryder." I took her cold hand in mine, holding it close to my lips. Suddenly, I felt her fingers move. "Jolene? Baby, I'm here! You're safe."

Her eyelids fluttered and her eyes tried to focus. "Ryder," she whispered. "Am I dreaming?"

"No, I'm here." I gathered her into my arms and held her tightly. She wrapped her arms loosely around my neck. "I'm so glad you're okay," I murmured as I kissed her cheek.

I heard a cough behind me. "Boss," Mason said. "The cops are here. We're going to fill them in. Do you need me to call an ambulance for either of you?"

"Yeah, I want them to check her out. I'll be okay."

Jolene sat back and looked at me. "Ryder, you're bleeding." She gently touched my cheek.

"I'm fine. I just need to make sure you are." I brushed back the hair from her eyes and saw her eyes fill with tears.

"I'm so sorry. I thought I was doing the best thing for everyone," she said softly.

I kissed her forehead. "It was most definitely not the best for everyone…and I would have had to go right over to Italy and drag you back home where you belong."

I looked down the aisle to see a couple of police officers come onto the plane. Jolene heard them and turned to me. "Ryder, I need to talk to Marco before they take him."

"Can you stand and walk?" I asked as she tried to get up.

"Yes, I think so." With me gripping her tightly around the waist, she threw her arm over my shoulder. As we walked up the aisle toward him, Marco deliberately averted his gaze.

Mason was interrogating him. "So, besides kidnapping, were you behind this stalking business, as well?" He asked as Marco squirmed in his seat.

He looked at him warily. "I don't know what you're talking about!"

Mason grew angry. "Cut the crap. I know you had someone watching her. We've already talked to him."

His eyes grew wide. "I knew I shouldn't have trusted him! Drake is an idiota and cost me a lot of money. Besides, he was more than willing to do what I wanted."

Jolene stared him down. "Marco, you make me sick. You would have hurt or killed me or my sister just to get out of debt? Giada left you her fortune because she loved you and respected you. Maybe she even hoped we'd end up together one day, but you ruined that when your greed got the best of you."

He dropped his head. "Jolene, I need the money. I need the money!" He wailed as he began thrashing around.

Shaking her head, she said, "I pity you, Marco. And, if you need money so badly, you could start by selling this stupid plane!"

He shook his head. "It's not mine. I leased it," he mumbled.

"With a disgusted look on her face, she said, "So, everything about you is a lie. I'm sorry, but I can't stay here. I can't stand the sight of you!"

I helped Jolene from the plane, and despite her objections had the EMTs check her out. Darryl drove up with Olivia, who ran straight to her sister's side. Jolene got the all clear from the EMTs as I walked over to join them. Meanwhile, the police got statements from everyone and arrested Marco for Olivia's kidnapping. Together, we watched them lead him in handcuffs to the police car

Joey walked over to us. "Boss, do you need me to take Ms. Anderson home?" He asked nodding his head toward Olivia, with more than a little interest in his eyes.

I laughed. "That's up to her."

"You gonna be okay?" She asked Jolene.

With a nod, Jolene took me by the arm. "Yes, Ryder's going to take care of me."

Olivia nodded and taking Joey by the arm, said with a brilliant smile, "So, tell me about yourself."

As they walked away, Jolene smiled. She looked up at me and said softly, "Thank you, Ryder…for everything." I didn't say a word, just pulled her to me, my lips finding hers. Her body molded to mine, and I held her tightly, never wanting to let go. Holding her close, I led her to the truck and helped her in. As I climbed into the driver's seat, her hand sought mine and linked it tightly. "I shouldn't have tried to handle everything on my own," she said softly.

I brought her hand to my lips and kissed it gently. "It's okay, you're safe, that's all that matters."

"Ryder, take me home," she whispered.

Our eyes met and nothing more needed to be said.

Chapter 17

Jolene

The wait was killing me. The drive back to Ryder's seemed as if it took forever. My heart was pounding out of my chest, and I prayed he didn't notice my sweaty palm. Every nerve in my body was tingling with anticipation.

As we drove, I closed my eyes and relived my close call at the airport. When I'd arrived at the airport, the pilot had been waiting at the entry gate with security, and they'd waved me right in. I'd followed him to the plane, anxiously searching for any sign of Olivia. Marco had appeared on the steps with a sadistic grin on his face, and I instantly regretted my rash decision but also knew this was the only way to save Olivia. As I climbed from the truck, he ran to me and tightly grabbed my arm as if he were afraid I'd run away. The feeling of helplessness was overwhelming, but I'd put on my best smile and told him that I still cared about him, and I wasn't going to try to leave. Seeing that I was complying, he'd relaxed his grip just a little but still kept a firm hold on me as he led me up the steps onto the plane. Olivia was locked in the bathroom, and as she heard my voice, she started pounding on the door.

"Look, you ass! Let me out of here, right NOW!" She screamed.

I called out, "Olivia, it's going to be okay."

"Jolene! What are you doing?" Marco just curled his lip into a sinister smile. When he opened the door, Olivia tumbled out, eyes wild. When she saw me, relief flooded her face but was quickly replaced with the realization that I wasn't there with anyone else. "No!" She cried. "Don't do it! He's crazy!"

The last comment riled Marco, and he pushed me down into a seat then grabbed her roughly by the arm. He growled, "Give Ryder a message. Tell him, I always get what I want. He loses!" She was crying and it was killing me, but I had to make her see that this was the best way.

Softly and calmly, I said, "It's okay, Liv. I want to do this. I'll be all right. He won't hurt me. I'm valuable to him." Marco, pleased that I was so accommodating, nodded in agreement.

"See, Sorellina, it's something she wants, yes?" His smug expression had sickened me and his reference to her as 'little sister', something Giada had called me, made it worse. She'd thrashed in his grip, her eyes pleading with me not to go but this was the only way my friends and family would be safe.

My eyes pleading, I begged Marco to let her go. "Look, you have what you want. You have me. Please let her leave." As he'd considered it, I took the opportunity to assure her. "Liv, just go. I'll be fine. I love you and please, tell everyone else I love them too." Turning to Marco, I said, "Would you please make sure she gets back to the airport safely, please?" I'd surprised myself with my steady, even tone.

His eyes had softened when I spoke to him so sweetly. "Si, I'll make sure." He'd tugged her down the short length of the plane, then at the door said something I couldn't hear. I gasped as he shoved her out the door but had taken a deep sigh of relief as I saw her running across the tarmac to safety. Marco, however, never stepped off the plane. He'd obviously thought it was a trick to get him to leave me alone so I could escape.

"You were supposed to make sure she was safe!" I'd cried. "How could you do that?

With a dismissive shake of his head, he'd sneered, "I have more important things to take care of. He'd stroked my cheek with the back of his hand. "Cara mia. You will grow to love me again. Once we're away from here…" He paused. "I only hope he hasn't had what's mine."

Coolly, I'd responded. "Marco, if you think this marriage is going to be anything other than on paper, you're sadly mistaken. Whether or not I've been with Ryder is frankly none of your business but as for you ever having me again, it's never going to happen!"

His eyes had narrowed as my words sunk in. He began pacing angrily, his jaw tightly clenched. With his back to me, he reached for something then before I could react, I felt a prick on my neck. Within moments, my fingers began to tingle, my vision blurred and that was the last thing I remembered until I heard Ryder calling my name.

I'd been so relieved to see Ryder. I was sure I wouldn't see him again but he was there, kissing me and holding me. As my head cleared, everything that had happened came rushing back and I knew I needed to speak to Marco. Gone was the man I'd cared for. In his place was a horrible, twisted person and seeing him for what he was, gave me the courage to speak my mind and get the closure I needed.

After Ryder walked me to the ambulance, Olivia came running up, her eyes scanning me. "What happened?" She'd asked holding me at arm's length. "Are you okay? Did he hurt you?"

"No, he didn't hurt me. He drugged me with something but I'll be okay. I really think in his own twisted way he still loved me."

She'd frowned. "I didn't want to leave you. If I could have kicked his ass myself, I would have. You know I've always been the scrappy one."

Laughing, I'd hugged her tightly. "I know, Liv. You're my hero."

She'd shaken her head. "No, I'm an idiot who managed to get herself kidnapped."

"Olivia, you are not an idiot. Marco had inside information on everything you did from the doorman, Drake," Ryder said as he wrapped his arms around the two of us. "Are you girls okay?"

I sighed leaning against him. "I am now." I was so relieved Marco would soon be out of my life, hopefully for good.

Joey had approached and quietly asked if he could escort Olivia home. I'd noticed them making eye contact on several occasions and there was definite chemistry between them. Olivia quickly grabbed Joey's arm then allowed him to lead her to his truck. I was grateful to the amazing people who had come to my rescue.

The police car drove away with Marco sulking in the back seat, and it was as if a huge weight lifted off of me. As it disappeared into the night, Ryder didn't say anything, just pulled me into his arms. Our eyes locked and as he leaned in, I could feel the whisper of his breath against my cheek. My lips parted in anticipation. One hand held me tightly by my waist and the other trailed up my back to cup the nape of my neck. My eyes fluttered closed as he captured my mouth with his. His lips were warm and gentle and as we kissed, I knew I never wanted it to end.

We finally did have to come up for air but when I looked into his eyes, I knew this was just the beginning. Without a word, he took my hand and led me to the truck. Once I was safely inside, he climbed into the driver's seat and immediately my hand sought his.

With the feel of his kiss still lingering on my lips, I realized I wanted more. I also knew what that would lead to. I needed him. "Ryder, take me home," I whispered.

With a nod, he'd cranked the truck, entwined his fingers with mine, and we drove to his house. As we pulled into the driveway, he opened my car door then scooped me up and carried me to the porch. After quickly unlocking the front door and gently kicking it open, he carried me into the house. He set me down and without hesitation, he cradled my face with his hands and kissed me again. His lips were demanding making my body burn with desire. He backed me against the door, his taut muscles straining under his t-shirt. My hands sought the hem of his shirt, and I yanked it quickly over his head. My fingers traced the contours of his solid chest and rock-hard abs. "Jolene…" he groaned against my mouth.

My lips curled into a smile at his reaction. "What do you want, Ryder?" I teasingly whispered against his lips.

He groaned again, his tongue dancing playfully with mine. My heart was thundering in my chest, my breath coming in short bursts.

He tangled one hand into my hair as he gripped my waist tightly with the other. He broke the kiss only to move to my neck which I arched to allow better access. His teeth tugged at my earlobe while his breath was hot against my skin. I felt his hand slide under my t-shirt and in one quick motion, he'd pulled it off and dropped it to the floor. His eyes devoured me taking in my lacy pink bra. He hooked his finger under the strap and eased it off of my shoulder, baring it to his kisses. At that moment, I wanted to rip the rest of our clothes off right there, but he slowed down leaving me puzzled.

Seeing my disappointment, he leaned in and whispered, "I want this to be special and the foyer is not my idea of special."

He effortlessly scooped me up again to carry me up the stairs, and I could feel the heat from his skin against mine. He carried me into the master bedroom which was only illuminated by the moonlight streaming through the blinds. He gently lay me onto the soft folds of the comforter on the bed before joining me. As I looked into his eyes, I could almost feel the love washing over me. I couldn't resist the flames of desire that consumed me. Sitting up, I threaded my fingers into his hair and drew his mouth to mine. As we kissed, I nudged him onto his back. My hair cascaded around us, but I felt him pull it back. "I don't want to miss a thing," he said before he pulled me down into another feverish kiss. His hands caressed my skin and slowly, peeled my bra away leaving nothing between us. He smiled as he traced his fingers down my bare skin leaving my body tingling.

Every touch, every kiss was full of desire and within moments, we'd shed the last of our clothes allowing us the freedom to explore and pleasure each other. Our kisses deepened and became more demanding. I was impatient and he could tell. With a wicked grin he rolled me onto my back, feathering my bare skin with kisses. My hands grasped his face pulling him face to face with me. "Now...I want you now," I whispered.

When our bodies joined, I gasped with the feeling of overwhelming passion. We made love with abandon, "You feel so good," he murmured.

Looking into his eyes and touching his face, I whispered, "I—I love you."

He breathed a sigh. "I love you, too. Baby, I always have." His eyes locked on mine as we moved in perfect rhythm until we both spiraled out of control then came breathlessly crashing down, our bodies spent. Clutching each other tightly, neither of us wanted to let go and for a long time, we didn't. We just lay together tangled in each other's arms.

When I finally found my breath, all I could say was, "Incredible."

He grinned. "That's exactly what I was thinking!"

As he pulled me tighter to him, I lay my head against his chest feeling the tickle of his chest hair against my cheek. He kissed the top of my head and with his heartbeat drumming in my ear, I fell asleep.

We woke up to our phones ringing simultaneously. Ryder grabbed his phone and handed me mine. His showed his dad calling, and mine was Olivia. He climbed from bed and threw on a t-shirt and shorts while I clutched the sheet around me. He mouthed he was going to grab us something to drink and eat, then left as he called his dad back. I could hear him talking as he went downstairs.

I listened to Olivia's voicemail, which was pretty much full of 'Where are you?' and 'What are you guys doing?' I called her back, and she answered almost immediately.

"About time!" She huffed.

"I'm sorry, we just woke up." By the time I realized what I'd just said, she was squealing with delight.

"Whoo hoo, sis! I knew it was going to happen sooner or later."

I laughed. "Well, I guess I'm not as smart as you."

"Nobody is!" she chuckled. "Seriously though, I think you're perfect for each other. Ryder's always loved you."

I hugged my knees to my chest. "Liv, he makes me feel like no one else exists. Is that crazy?"

She laughed again. "No, that's just true love. Remember the fairy tales, Jolene. That's how they all live happily ever after!"

Ryder came into the room carrying a tray bearing fresh fruit and two tall glasses of ice cold water. He set the tray on the side table then sat on the edge of the bed to give me a kiss. The look in his eye told me to cut this call short.

"Hey, Liv…I need to go. Ryder just brought breakfast."

She snorted. "Sure, is that what you're calling it? Go get it! Surface when you're ready. Love you!"

I smiled. She was such a nut. "Love you too!"

I was just about to hang up when I heard her say, "Give Ryder my love!"

He heard her and shouted, "Love you too, Liv!"

He took the phone from my hand then tossed it over onto the oversized chair in the corner. "No more interruptions," he growled as he slowly pulled down the sheet. "Lay back," he whispered. I did as he asked, and he took a strawberry from the tray and held it to my lips. It was bright red and looked delicious. I opened my mouth to take a bite but at the last moment, he moved it and kissed me softly.

I threw out my lower lip in a pout. "No fair," I said, my voice husky with desire. "You're a tease."

His eyes grew wide with amusement. "Tease?" He said with a mischievous smile. "Is someone trying to tell me they're hungry?"

With hooded eyes, I answered. "Hungry for you."

He placed the strawberry back onto the plate. His mouth captured mine, and the fruit was completely forgotten for the next hour.

Chapter 18

Jolene

"If you kids stand on those seats, I'll sell you to the circus!" MaryBeth said with her hands on her hips.

Ryder's friends MaryBeth and Seth were visiting and Ryder had gotten us all VIP seats for the Panther's football game. One of his new clients was a wide receiver for the team who had been hassled by an overzealous fan. He was so grateful for the protection that he offered Ryder the seats and so he just had to call Seth and give him the good news. MaryBeth stood behind the oldest two, Daniel and Landry, and said, "Uncle Ryder got us these cool tickets so you'd better behave or else we'll get kicked out of the stadium."

The kids turned and looked at Ryder with wide eyes. "Is that true?" Daniel asked.

Ryder looked at MaryBeth and saw the look that Seth had often described as the 'do as I do, say as I say' look. "Yep, the big security guys will come and take you out to the parking lot." They both immediately dropped into the seats and began pointing at the brightly colored big screen televisions. John, the youngest, was sitting contentedly with his dad, chattering away. There weren't too many words in his vocabulary yet but he still managed to talk nonstop.

MaryBeth came over to sit by me. Looking over at Seth, she said with a smile, "He just got home from two months in leadership school. He's got some Daddy time to catch up on."

Seth was obviously thrilled to have his kids with him but within a few minutes, he was looking over to MaryBeth for help. "Babe? Help a guy out?"

She waved and called out, "You got this! You deal with guns and explosives every day. You can take care of three kids!"

Seth laughed. "You think ALC prepared me for dealing with these monkeys?"

MaryBeth shrugged her shoulders. "I figure if it'll teach you how to handle a bunch of Army guys, it should work for our brood." She settled back and pointing to Ryder, she said, "You know, he's really a great guy."

I nodded and smiled. "He's definitely a keeper."

Seth started hooting as the big screen showed the teams running out onto the field. The guys became so enthralled with explaining the game that I had to laugh. Ryder knew I loved football and had watched a lot of it when I was younger, but I could see it pleased him to explain what was happening during the game to me.

Finally, it was halftime and I was ready for a bathroom break and some more yummy popcorn but when I grabbed my wallet to leave, Ryder grasped my arm. "Where are you going?"

I laughed. "Seriously? I think I can go to the ladies room without a bodyguard."

He looked distressed. "Jolene, you can't leave now."

"What's wrong?" I asked as he led me to the edge of the box overlooking the field. Suddenly on the big screen, I realized that the camera was pointed to us. "Wha—" I spun to find Ryder on one knee.

"Jolene," he said taking my now shaking hand. "I love you and want to spend my life with you. Will you marry me? Please make me the happiest man on earth and say yes." He pulled a box from behind his back and opened it to reveal a beautiful pear shaped diamond ring.

The crowd was going wild as I stood there like a complete idiot, totally dumbfounded. We'd talked about marriage but never seriously. The eight months we'd been together had been amazing, and I was hoping this would happen but I never expected it in such a public place!

I realized that everyone was staring at me waiting for my answer. Tears began streaming down my cheeks as I nodded and managed to say, "Yes!"

Ryder slipped the ring, which fit perfectly, onto my finger. He then stood and lifted me into his arms, spinning me around as he pumped his fist in the air. The crowd erupted in applause and the giant screen flashed the message 'Congratulations, Ryder and Jolene!'

Ryder set me down then kissed me, much to the amusement of Daniel and Landry, who stood giggling nearby.

Seth shook Ryder's hand and MaryBeth gave me a warm hug. "Congrats! Now you're definitely stuck with us!"

I looked down at the sparkling diamond on my left hand and smiled. She grasped my hand and looked at my ring. "Wow! I had to be married five years before I graduated from the chip. You got the rock on the first go round!" She called out to Ryder. "Was this the three month's salary diamond? If so, you're making way too much being a babysitter for those celebs."

Ryder grinned. "We looked at rings once and she forbid me from ever getting the one I suggested. She said she didn't want to wear a lethal weapon."

MaryBeth released my hand with a sigh. "Seth, I think after you get out of the Army, you need to go into business with Ryder. I could grow to love a big ring."

Seth walked over to MaryBeth and gave her a kiss. "You know. You're the best wife my money at the time could buy!" She smacked him on the arm but the smile they exchanged said it all.

Ryder came over and threw his arm around my shoulder. "So, now all you have to do is plan a wedding and we're all set."

MaryBeth smiled. "I love weddings. Do you want to do a big one or just a small one? Seth and I did the courthouse wedding but I always dreamed of having the white dress and all the festivities."

My head was spinning. "I don't really know. I think whatever Ryder wants is fine with me."

Seth gave Ryder a thumbs up. "Got her whipped already? I'm impressed, man. I should have trained this one better." He swatted MaryBeth on the rear as he said it, and she rolled her eyes.

"Right, Seth. We know who wears the pants in that family," Ryder said laughing. He turned to me and said, "I want to marry you anywhere, whether it's in front of a judge at the courthouse or in the biggest chapel in Charlotte. You give me a time and a place and I'll be there."

The rest of the game, I tried to pay attention but my mind kept wandering to the proposal and the exciting but daunting task of planning a wedding. After the game was over, we said goodbye to Seth and Marybeth and promised to let them know what our final plans were.

When we got back to the house, I called my parents and gave them the good news. Neither of them sounded surprised and when I questioned them about it, they told me that Ryder had already been by to tell them of his intentions first. My parents had given him their blessing and had been ordered to keep it secret until the big day. His parents were elated as well. Olivia called me and the ear-splitting shriek that greeted me when I answered left me momentarily deaf in that ear. After switching to the other one, I could hear her jabbering away.

"Oh we *have* to have a fall wedding! It's so darn hot here any other time. Can you imagine how beautiful the pictures would be with all the leaves turning? Of course, I'll be the maid of honor but I'll be willing to share with Lucinda if you want, because I really like her and understand with her being your best friend and all but I'm your sister so that should make it automatic!" When she finally took a breath, I assured her that of course she'd be my maid of honor, and I also intended to ask Lucinda.

I really liked the idea of a fall wedding, so Ryder and I chose Saturday, October 12th as our official date giving us just about a year of preparation. In addition to planning a wedding, I was also busy preparing for the launch of another clothing line. It had been picked up by a major high end retailer, and my designs were going to be all over the world. I'd intended to stay small, but with Olivia as my business manager, things had grown like crazy. I was loving every minute of it.

Ryder had over a dozen employees now with the original team still intact. His business was so successful in the Charlotte area that he actually had to turn down requests. One he did take on, with tongue in cheek, was Rusty MacNeil. Rusty's former security team ended up taking his motorhome on a drunken joyride into Lake Lloyd at Daytona International Speedway. He fired them all on the spot and called Ryder for help. He sent a team on the road with him, which was also there to protect Ryanne, Gage, and the newest MacNeil on the way.

Lucinda had returned to London for Fashion week but within a month had called in tears after a particularly rough day working with Fazon. Right then, I asked her to come work with me as a partner and she immediately accepted. We arranged it so she could work in both the US and the UK.

Ryanne and Rusty generously offered the use of their home on Lake Norman for our wedding venue. At first, I'd suggested having it at what I still called 'Ryder's house', but he deemed it too small to entertain properly so I agreed to the Lake Norman site. The view really was magnificent and the security was going to be much easier to handle, as Ryder pointed out several times.

My brother Ethan had graduated from high school and was doing culinary studies in Paris. He promised he'd be home for the big event regardless if it was in the middle of a semester.

I finished working on my latest collection then began working on the wedding plans. With my creative juices flowing, I designed the bridesmaid dresses in a deep bronze making a different style for each of my co-maids of honor, Olivia and Lucinda. They were thrilled with the colors I'd chosen because they truly worked for each of them despite their unique coloring. Ryder chose as his best man, his dad and as a groomsman, his brother Carter. They were going to be dressed in classic black tailored suits with simple black ties. The only thing I needed was my wedding dress and that was where I hit a wall. I'd designed hundreds of dresses but couldn't visualize my own.

I'd been having a particularly rough day and was in my office with the door closed when I heard a tiny knock. Olivia peeped in. "Hey sis...there's someone here to see you."

I sighed. "Okay, send them in." I rubbed my temples then put on my best smile.

The door opened and in walked a man who looked like an older version of Marco. "Signorina Anderson, I am Giuseppe Rinaldo." He extended his hand but I stood there like a statue, frozen in shock. "Mi dispiace, it seems I've startled you, yes?"

Taking a shaky breath, I said, "Please, don't be sorry. It just caught me off guard." I held my hand to him and he quickly brought it to his lips. "It's nice to finally meet you," I said inviting him to sit.

He smiled. "Si, it is good for us to meet. First of all, please let me apologize for my son. He confessed everything he did to you. His mother and I were shocked to hear how desperate he had become."

I was dumbfounded. "Excuse me, Signore Rinaldo, but what would make him tell you this?"

He shook his head and shrugged. "Perhaps being in prison in Italy has changed him, who knows."

I gasped. "I didn't know he was in Italy!"

"Si, when he was arrested for the kidnapping, they found he had many, many outstanding charges in Italy. They sent him back to be punished. He serves several years for his crimes but has promised

God and his mother that he has changed his ways." His eyes grew misty. "He's our only son and it is so painful to see him there but I see a new light in his eyes. Perhaps, this was for the best."

"Signore, may I ask what brings you here?" I asked, still reeling from the news about Marco.

He stood and walked to the door. "Antonio, please bring it in." A moment later, a huge man walked in carrying a garment bag. With his towering height, he had no problem hanging it on the top of the door. With a nod, he turned and left us alone.

"My sister, Giada, loved you like a daughter. She had hoped Marco would be a good match for you and dreamed of seeing you get married one day. But she also knew he was a man and men can be unpredictable. We found something for you among her personal things. Her wish was that it be a surprise for your wedding. I watch the entertainment television and they showed you and your fiancé were soon to marry so I knew it must come to you and whether or not you use it is up to you." He unzipped the bag and as I stepped closer, I felt my heart begin to race. Inside was the most beautiful wedding gown I'd ever seen. It was made of vintage Italian lace in off-white. I laughed as I felt tears sting my eyes. Giada and I had always fought over wedding dresses. She believed they should be traditional white and I preferred them to be off-white. I could almost picture her with a silly grin saying, "Jolene, you must wear the white, unless you are a bad girl." I'd always bristled at that comment calling her old-fashioned which only made her laugh harder.

Giuseppe pulled the dress from the bag to reveal its amazing details. It was a mermaid style with dainty spaghetti straps and a sweetheart neckline. Floor-length with a small train, it was perfect in every possible detail. I stared at the dress, not believing my eyes. "Signore, it's beautiful. The only thing I worry about is…well, will it fit me?"

He smiled and I saw a glimpse of Marco when we'd first met. They had the same sweet smile but sadly, Marco's had become twisted and cold. "Well, Signorina Anderson, we need to find out. I will get your assistant to help you."

He walked out and a few seconds later, Olivia came bursting in. "Oh my God! Is that what I think it is?" She cried.

Biting my lip to fight the tears, I nodded. "Yes, it's a present from Giada. Can you believe it?"

She shook her head as she walked around the dress. "I'm amazed, it's perfect. Come on, let's get you into it."

I hesitated. "What if it's too small? I don't think I could take the disappointment."

Olivia looked at me and then the dress. "Looks like a match to me. Get out of your clothes now, woman!"

She ran to the door and turned the lock as I slipped out of my blouse and skirt and then she rushed to hold the dress for me. As we slid it over my head, the feel of the lace and tulle was so soft, it felt like a cloud billowing around me. Olivia pulled it down and then reached behind me to zip it.

"Is there a huge gap or am I going to have to go on a water diet?" I asked holding my breath.

"Neither! This baby is going to zip just fine." She straightened the back then zipped it right up. "Jolene, take a look at yourself. It's incredible."

I turned and walked to the wall of mirrors in my studio and what I saw took my breath away. It was perfect. "How—how did she do this?" I whispered.

Olivia rested her head on my shoulder as she gazed at my reflection. "She loved you, that's how. You have a very special angel, Jolene."

I felt an ugly cry coming on so I took deep breaths to stop it so I wouldn't risk messing up my beautiful gown. "Grazie di cuore, Giada," I said lifting my eyes toward heaven. "You were my family, my friend and always will be in my heart."

I heard a sniffle and turned to see Olivia dabbing her eyes. "That was so beautiful."

Olivia ran out to her office and brought Giuseppe in to see the dress. "Bellisimo!" He cried. I hugged him and thanked him for being so kind. I also told him I'd be praying for Marco and his new life.

Later that night, when I came home, Ryder was sitting on the front porch. "How was your day, beautiful?" He asked, rising to kiss me.

The dress was going to remain a surprise until the actual wedding day.

"It was perfect," was all I could say.

Epilogue

September...

Ryder

The morning of our wedding had been beautiful. We were blessed that everyone in our families could attend and share our special day with us. When Jolene finally walked down the aisle on the arm of her father, Jay, I literally lost my breath. Words couldn't describe how beautiful she was. She joined me at the altar and when she slipped her hand in mine, I felt a tiny electric shock. When I looked at her with surprise, she just grinned. Jolene had asked Tyler to perform the ceremony as he was now ordained, he enthusiastically agreed. The ceremony began and I focused on every detail committing it to memory.

Soon, he came to the part where we were to say our vows. Jolene and I had gone back and forth about having standard ones or making up our own. I won and she had to write her own vows.

Tyler began with me. I turned to Jolene and looking deep into her big blue eyes, I said, "Jolene, today you make me the happiest man in the world because today, you promise to share the rest of your life with me. Not many men can say they've known the love of their life for their *entire* life, but I can. You've been my friend, my lover and now, you'll be my wife…my life partner. Together, we'll build a home and God willing, have some children to make our lives complete. I pledge my love to you today and always."

He then motioned for Jolene to say hers. She hesitated, and I felt her hands trembling. She swallowed hard, took a deep breath and said, "Ryder, you have always been so important to me, as my friend and now as my husband. I knew from the first moment I laid eyes on you that you were special and I loved you from the beginning but sometimes life takes you down a road away from those who are most important to you. I'm so glad that God brought us back together and that you didn't give up on making me see that the only place I need to be is by your side, forever. I love you, and I will for the rest of my days."

I gave her a huge smile and impatiently waited for the next step. Before Tyler could pronounce us man and wife, I jumped the gun and kissed her until she was breathless in my arms.

I scooped her into my arms and carried her down the aisle. The reception had been nothing short of epic. Ryanne insisted on having a photo booth, so we all dressed in funny hats and wigs and posed in some of the most ridiculously funny pictures I'd ever seen. Both sets of our grandparents had even joined in the fun with my grandma wearing a bright pink wig and a tiara. MaryBeth, Seth and the kids had come despite their worries that the kids would drive everyone crazy. They'd been concerned that the kids would mess up the wedding, but Jolene had thought of everything and had set up a bouncy house on the lawn so all the bigger kids could entertain themselves in it. John and Gage became fast friends making sand castles in the sandbox. Everything was just perfect.

The time came for everyone to say a few words and the first volunteer was my dad. He praised me for being a strong man and threatened to hurt me if I didn't take good care of his favorite girl. Jolene's dad spoke and told everyone that I was truly the only man worthy of his daughter. That made me tear up. Lucinda and Olivia stood and they basically told everyone that they knew we'd end up together, we just had to get our heads out of our arses. I laughed because I knew who'd come up with that part.

Finally, the party wound down after hours of dancing and lots of champagne. As we prepared to leave to go off on our honeymoon, our guests lined the path to my car to wish us a safe trip. I led Jolene toward the car and suddenly, we were surrounded by dozens of tiny bubbles. The guests were blowing them at us making Jolene giggle. "I didn't know about that," she whispered with a huge smile. We climbed into the car and as we pulled away, we could hear our dearest friends cheering us on.

I turned to my bride and smiled. "So, have you figured out where we're going yet?" I asked as I linked my hand in hers.

Shaking her head, she shrugged. "I really have no idea. It can't be too far. I know you won't leave the firm too long."

Eyebrows raised, I smiled. "Ah, you think you know me, but you don't."

We drove to the house where my first surprise was waiting. While we'd been gone for the wedding, I'd had workers come in and repaint the inside of the house to the colors I knew she'd like. Our bedroom had been transformed into a less austere, more warm and inviting space. Everything I'd had done was to make her feel like it was her home not just mine.

The second surprise was our suitcases sitting packed in the hallway. "Ryder, those aren't the bags I packed last night," she said with her hands on her hips. "What have you done?"

I strolled over to pick up a bag to take it to the car. "Well, I kinda repacked with some more appropriate clothing."

She frowned. "I tried to pack something for both warm and cold. Did I mess up?"

I smiled. "No, baby. You did fine. But when you're going to be gone for a month, you need a few more clothes."

Her mouth fell open. "A month? Ryder! Where are we going? And what about work?"

I grabbed some papers out of the drawer in the desk and handed them to her. "Lucinda's going to be handling everything while you're gone. Hurry up and change. The plane won't wait for us."

Her eyes scanned the pages and I could see the realization on her face. "Australia?!"

"The land down under. Yep, that's where we're headed." I swatted her on the backside. "Get a move on, Mrs. Brisson. Time's a-wastin'!"

I loaded the car and ran upstairs to change. She had changed but was sitting staring at the brochures. "Baby?" I said trying not to startle her.

She jumped just a little. "Sorry, I just can't believe you and I are going to Australia. I loved that country." A wistful smile came over her face, and I knew she was thinking of that last time she'd been with Giada.

She jumped to her feet, took me by the hand, and said as we dashed out the door, "Let's go have our happily ever after!"

And we did.

THE END

Coming soon

Book 2 in the Solitaire Series

www.ingramcontent.com/pod-product-compliance
Lightning Source LLC
Chambersburg PA
CBHW061606170626
46811CB00001B/336